570

D0992392

*Treegate's Raiders* ☆

Ariel Books by Leonard Wibberley

Fiction

*Treegate's Raiders*
*Sea Captain from Salem*
*Peter Treegate's War*
*John Treegate's Musket*
*Kevin O'Connor and the Light Brigade*
*The Wound of Peter Wayne*
*Deadmen's Cave*
*The King's Beard*

Non-fiction

*Wes Powell, Conqueror of the Grand Canyon*
*John Barry, Father of the Navy*
*The Life of Winston Churchill*
*The Epics of Everest*
*The Coronation Book*

☆ LEONARD WIBBERLEY

# *Treegate's Raiders* ☆

*Ariel Books · Farrar, Straus and Cudahy · New York*

Ariel Books, a division of
Farrar, Straus and Cudahy
Published simultaneously in Canada by
Ambassador Books, Ltd., Toronto
Manufactured in the United States of America
by H. Wolff

*Treegate's Raiders* ☆

It was the fall of the year 1780 and that war which had started higgledy-piggledy five years earlier with an untidy crackle of musketry at the villages of Concord and Lexington, and which had swept the North American continent from as far north as Quebec to as far south as Savannah, Georgia, had ground to a stalemate.

Neither side had won. Neither side had lost. Neither side seemed capable of any plan or action which would bring about a decision. It was indeed as if the only victors of this war were to be death and destruction —the burned-out houses in New York City, the burned-out plantations of the Carolinas, the neglected farms of eastern Pennsylvania and the bones of men lying unburied in the wilderness from the upper reaches of the Hudson to the swamps of South Carolina.

The news that came to the tall, patient and enduring man at the De Windt mansion, which was his headquarters at Tappan, New York, had been bad for weeks. He winced whenever a courier, splattered with mud or powdered with dust according to the season, flung into the barracks' yard outside headquarters shouting his credentials, with dispatches for the Commander-in-Chief. Such dispatches recently had contained nothing but disastrous news—the defeat of General Horatio Gates at Camden in South Carolina, which meant the final subduing of the southern colonies by the British, or the treachery of General Benedict Arnold who had planned to hand over West Point to the enemy. So it went.

The treachery of Arnold, one of his most brilliant officers, had shaken General Washington more than he was prepared to admit even to himself. His mind returned to it constantly so that now he wondered about other members of his staff—Wayne, Knox, Greene, Sullivan. They had, to be sure, all been with him since the earliest days. But so had Arnold, who had been present at the storming of Quebec in the first year of the war, and had personally led the climactic attack at Saratoga. Arnold would soon be appearing in the uniform of a British general, leading British troops against the Continentals he had but recently commanded.

To what extent then could Washington trust the others on his staff? And this thought had hardly occurred to him before he blushed with shame at it, and said aloud, "I should rather ask myself to what extent can my officers trust me? For after five years I have brought them no nearer to victory than they were when the first shot was fired."

There was a knock on the door and an aide entered. "Mr. John Treegate has just arrived, sir," he said, "and asks to see you at your convenience."

"Is he outside?" asked Washington. "Send him in right away. One moment. He will have ridden from Boston. Bring a dish of tea for him and lace it with New England rum."

The man who entered was caked with dirt from head to foot. He wore a riding coat which came down to his calves and the lower portions were thick with clay. His jack boots were so mired that the strap over the instep could not be seen and there was a blob of mud on the side of his prominent nose. There was a line across his forehead where the brim of his hat had rested. All below this line was dirty and all above clean, producing an effect that brought a trace of a smile to Washington's face.

"You've ridden hard," he said. "Bad news?" And he braced himself, sure that it would be bad.

John Treegate shook his head. He was an old man, or seemed old, for his face was lined, his eyebrows were bushy and white and his hair a kind of yellowing gray. He was struggling with the top button of his riding coat and while doing so he glanced at the door through which he had just entered to ensure that it was closed and then said, "The South."

"What of the South?" asked Washington, genuinely

puzzled. "The army is smashed in the South. The British are in command of Savannah, Charleston and Camden. The South is lost."

John Treegate shook his head. He had struggled out of his greatcoat revealing a neat suit of good brown worsted, for John Treegate had once been a Boston importer and the neatness of his peactime habits still clung to him. He was now the man of business of the continental cause, borrowing money wherever he could for the Continental Army, finding provisions, using his connections in France and the West Indies and Canada to round up a shipload of boots, a few thousand yards of cloth for uniforms, or five wagonloads of hay for the cavalry. Because of these activities, he was perhaps the only man other than Washington who was in touch with the needs on all fronts of the war, and also because of these activities, he had become the unofficial but nonetheless efficient head of the Continental Intelligence.

"Gates was routed at Camden and what is left of his army got to Charlotte, North Carolina," he said. "About eight hundred men and hardly a rifle or musket among them. But all over the South there are patriot bands springing up, attacking the British. If we move fast and get someone in the field to rally them, the South can be won back. But we must move now before the British crush these little bands altogether. They plan to do so by marching into North Carolina headed for Virginia and Pennsylvania."

"These are not rumors?" asked Washington. "You are sure of your source?"

"They are not rumors," said John Treegate. "My source is sure."

"And who is your source?"

"My son. Captain Peter Treegate of the Pennsylvania Line. He was with Gates at Camden. He has just returned with the latest word. He has been in contact with the leaders of the bands and they sent him here seeking help. They ask for a commander, weapons and a small force and they promise they will eventually regain the South."

At that moment the aide arrived carrying on a tray a dish of hot tea from which came the fragrant aroma of rum. Washington signalled the man to give the tea to John Treegate who took it gratefully, drinking so deeply and fast that his prominent nose disappeared for a few seconds in the depths of the dish. Washington watched with pleasure. He had a great fondness for this man who had fought side by side with him in another war a long time ago, when American militia and British regulars had, as allies, battled the French on the Heights of Abraham in Canada.

"Your son?" he said. "Is he with you?"

"Yes," said John Treegate. "He rode with me. He knows the Carolinas well. He was brought up there for some years by his foster father—the Maclaren of Spey. His training was of the frontier rather than of Boston." There was a touch of pride in John Treegate's voice that was not lost on George Washington. "We were together, he and I, at Bunker Hill," he added.

Washington turned to the aide. "Ask Captain Peter Treegate to come in," he said.

Washington was a tall man, topping six feet readily, but so well proportioned that it was only when he stood beside a man of normal size that his huge physique became obvious. The man who now entered the room was of the same size as the Commander-in-Chief though many years his junior. He was clad in a hunting shirt and leggings and had moccasins on his feet. His chest was broad and flat and his face as brown as a rock.

It was a young face but not immature—the face of a man who had endured much hardship but had survived to be the better for it. He wore his hair long in a queue down the back of his hunting shirt. He had a bold, unbending look to him. He carried as a sidearm a tomahawk in his belt and saluted Washington by putting his hand upon this and saying, "Captain Peter Treegate, Pennsylvania Line." It was the formal salute of an officer who was uncovered and Washington who liked the military courtesies nodded his approval.

"Be seated, Captain," he said indicating a chair. "Your father tells me you have news of the situation in the southern colonies. I have little. Tell me the situation."

"I will tell you what I believe you know already, sir," said Peter, "and then I will add what I believe is new.

"First, then, as you know, we have no army in the Carolinas or Georgia. When I left there were eight hundred, mostly unarmed, men at Charlotte under General Gates. They are deserting daily, though the deserters are mostly of the militia. The men of the Continental Line—from Pennsylvania, Virginia and Delaware for the greater part—are standing firm. They will not desert. But these men have no confidence in General Gates and their morale is low. If they do not get a replacement for General Gates, they will leave and return to their homes.

"However, the British defeat of Gates has not had the effect on the general population of the southern states that Cornwallis expected. He thought there would be dismay and surrender. Instead there is anger and rebellion. Too many farms and plantations have been burned to the ground, and too many churches too, for the people to accept defeat and British rule."

"Churches?" interrupted General Washington. "I didn't think the British made a practice of burning churches."

"Not the British regulars, sir," said Peter. "But the Tories—the local people siding with the British. They are settling old scores by burning non-conforming churches. In some cases they have freed slaves, armed them, and incited them against their masters. They've gone about in bands looting and marauding and destroying settlements. In parts of North Carolina there are vast areas, once settled and prosperous, that are now in ruins and there is hardly a soul living in them. A lot of old feuds are being settled by licensed murder. And the British, to reward those who took their side, are turning a blind eye to looting. In short the British have done just what they should not have done. Instead of pacifying the land after their victory, they have stirred it up against themselves, and bands have been formed spontaneously throughout the Carolinas to attack British outposts and forts and supply columns."

"Who is leading these bands?" asked Washington.

"Men of whom you have perhaps never heard," said Peter. "Francis Marion who is called The Swamp Fox is the biggest among them. But there is also Nollichucky Jack Scott and Pickens and Sumter. They live in the hills and swamps, raid the British lines and then retire. I was with Nollichucky Jack before I came north to report. We hanged three Tories the day I left."

"Hanged them, sir?" said Washington sharply, flushing with quick anger. "There was a trial, I trust?"

"We hanged them," said Peter slowly, "on a tree outside a farmhouse they had burned to the ground. The witnesses against them were dead inside—a woman and three children, the youngest about two years of age. They were burned to death. It is that kind of war, sir. A war of families against armed raiders and partisans against regulars. It is civil war, bloodier than has ever been seen in the northern colonies. In New England there was revolution—in the South there is civil war, patriots against Tories, the latter armed by the British."

There was a wood fire burning in the grate of the room in which they were sitting, for the day was cold and the river damp lay heavily around the house. The fire burned only sullenly, giving off a little smoke, the logs covered with gray ash. General Washington got up and put the sole of his boot against one of the logs and pressed on it. The log broke and immediately burst into flames. He seemed pleased with the effects and turning from the fire faced the other two.

"What do you want of me?" he asked. The question was simply put, as if he had a great desire to be of use and was anxious to do whatever he could.

"A leader who can put some heart back into the remnants of the army," said Peter. "One who knows how to co-operate with the partisans—with Marion and Nolli-chucky Jack and Pickens. Arms for the regulars. Cavalry. Whatever you can spare."

There were a few seconds of silence and when Washington spoke again he seemed not so much to be talking to the others but to be thinking aloud.

"New York is the key," he said. "All our efforts together with those of the French must be bent on driving the British from Manhattan Island. If that can be done, we will have freed our major cities—Boston, Philadelphia, New York. These cities—the port cities—are what matter. What happens elsewhere is only on the fringe and will have little effect on eventual victory."

He said this with his big head bent low, staring at the carpet before him. And when he had finished he looked up directly at the younger Treegate and asked, "You have any comment, Captain Treegate?"

"Yes, sir," said Peter. "I think you are wrong."

John Treegate was shocked at the frankness of the comment and looked sharply from his son to Washington and back again but said nothing.

"Why do you think I am wrong?" asked Washington almost humbly.

"Because you think America is a city and America is not a city," said Peter. "It is a country. If you take the cities away, the country will still be there. When the fighting in the back country dies down; when the men there won't fight any more, won't support the war any more, then the country is lost, even if you take New York by storm. And if you captured New York tomorrow and left North and South Carolina and Georgia to the British, you would have lost, not won the war, sir.

"The little towns and hamlets of America, places like Concord and Lexington and Trenton and Princeton, are where the war is to be decided. You knew that when you were on the South Bank of the Delaware in the winter of Seventy-Six, and asked me whether I thought the river could be crossed.* I hope you haven't forgotten it now because if you have, you have forgotten what made you a great general."

"You are too bold, boy," snapped John Treegate to his son. "You should learn respect. You do not talk to your Commander-in-Chief in this fashion."

"I am bold, sir, because I come of a bold nation," replied Peter Treegate. "If I have to speak with discretion not saying plainly what I have in mind, then I am wasting my time talking and General Washington's time in listening. There is no disrespect in saying honestly what I believe."

"I agree," said Washington. "Tell me what else you have in mind."

"There is a stalemate in the war now, sir," said Peter. "Clinton holds New York City and will hardly venture forth to fight. You cannot take New York. It is a fortress surrounded by the moat of the Hudson River. If I were

* (See PETER TREEGATE'S WAR)

Clinton, I would stay in New York and let your army rot from inactivity and dwindle away.

"In the south, Cornwallis is master of the land. Unless some action is taken, some help sent, the people in the Carolinas will become dispirited and the cause will be lost.

"The stalemate favors the British and threatens us. It must be broken. The place to break it is in the southern colonies. Let us entice Cornwallis into the swamps and the wilderness by a series of raids. Let us attack him and withdraw, attack once more and withdraw once more. Let us goad him to action and bleed him little by little while our army improves and his dwindles. Send a commander who can lead the regulars in North Carolina. Let this commander co-operate with the partisans. Revive the war, sir, on the only front where it can be revived—the southern front. Rebellions are won by rebellion and not by inactivity. If we are not active now, our rebellion may wither to nothing."

To this Washington made no immediate reply. He was going over in his mind the whole course of the war, now approaching its sixth year, trying to select those victories which in his view had been the most important.

The British surrender of Boston, ringed in by a vast Continental Army, had been a great victory. But far greater had been the dash he had made across the Delaware in midwinter with a few thousand men at his back to raid the towns of Trenton and Princeton. Again the country had rejoiced when the British were compelled to evacuate Philadelphia. But far more important had been the surrender of Burgoyne's army in the Hudson wilderness, which was the result of a series of nagging battles that had incapacitated Burgoyne and his Redcoats.

Was it possible that this young captain was right? Was he wrong in thinking that the war would be won or lost in a great culminating battle to capture New York City?

The little battles . . . what a list of them there was. Concord, Lexington, Bunker Hill, Brooklyn Heights, White Plains, Trenton, Princeton, Brandywine, Monmouth, Springfield. They went on and on. But by a series of such little battles he had bloodied and humbled the greatest military power in Europe. Perhaps he was wrong now to think of switching to grand strategy; the storming of a huge city like New York. That was European warfare, but this was America and warfare here was different. Yet New York must be contained and he could not move any great number of men into the southern theatre.

"How old are you, Captain?" he asked. The question surprised Peter Treegate. He thought for a moment in silence and said, "Twenty-one, sir."

"You were sixteen at Bunker Hill then?"

"Yes, sir."

Washington nodded. "I will think of what you have said, Captain," he said. "I will think deeply of it." And then he added slowly, "Alone," and he seemed in that moment immensely older.

When they had left, Washington stood looking at the door through which the young captain had passed. He thought that had he been blessed with a son of his own, that son might be just such a man as Peter Treegate. He felt a sense of nearness to him and wondered whether he had a sweetheart, or perhaps a wife, and was unhappy that he had not inquired into this.

## 2 ☆

A savage wind was slicing across the seaport of Salem, Massachusetts, bursting the gray Atlantic rollers in a fury of spray over the mole of the outer harbor. Inland, the wind ripped the branches of the chestnut and maple trees that dotted the streets of the town. Peace of God Manly, Captain in the Continental Navy and Commander of the Sloop of War *Defiance*, listened to the howling of the wind past the wooden shutters of his cottage windows and reflected in his solemn way on its significance.

The *Defiance* was in the inner harbor and was snug enough for he had anticipated this autumn storm. The day before had been pleasant but he had seen the sea gulls streaming inland, settling on the fields three and four miles from the shore and he knew the storm was coming. So he had sent down his topmasts and battened down the hatches and put out an additional bower anchor so his ship was as safe as could be contrived.

On the other hand, his gunner would certainly be drunk. The gunner's name was Simmons and he served a gun better than any man in the Continental Navy in the considered opinion of Peace of God Manly. But in the face of New England rum—or any spirits for that matter—Simmons was as defenseless as a baby. However often he vowed in his bouts of repentance never to touch another drop of spirits, he had to have but half an hour of idleness and he was off to the nearest tavern—the Blue Anchor, the Crown and Shield, the Rose and Leopard—and there drank himself insensible.

Peace of God had ordered the gunner to stay aboard the *Defiance* and Simmons had assured him with the sincerity of a man on his deathbed that he would. But with the ship idled by the storm and half the crew ashore with their families, Peace of God knew that the gunner's resolution would soon disappear and he would be at that moment in some taproom, drowning out the noise of the storm with a chorus of "Lillibulero" or "The Derby Ram" or some other heathenish song.

"If ever Satan had a poor mortal man in his toils, then Simmons is that man," said Peace of God aloud. "And sinner though I am myself, one of John Wesley's poor flock and all unworthy, yet must I try to save him. For we are brothers all, and who deserts his brother deserts himself, and so is lost."

His daughter, Nancy, was seated by the fire working on a quilt made of patches of various materials. She sat very erect at her work, having been taught that to lean back against the chair was to invite sloth, which was one of the deadliest of sins.

She made three neat stitches before she commented on her father's outburst. She did this because she had been taught never to speak immediately after another, but to allow an interval for reflection so that what she said would be seemly and sensible and not vain chatter. She had a delicate look to her, a fairness of hair and skin and bones that turned many a head in Salem when she walked through the town, though she was quite unconscious of her loveliness. Indeed, she had never seen her face in a mirror and so did not know what it looked like.

"It is a pity that Master Simmons is not married," she said at length. "I think a wife could handle him where a captain can't."

Peace of God looked at his daughter closely. She was eighteen years of age and he had recently become conscious of the fact that she was no longer a child and he ought to be seeking a husband for her. But he knew of no man in Salem to whom he would entrust her and, of them all, Simmons was the last. This talk of Simmons needing a wife disturbed him.

"Simmons would make no bargain for any woman," he said. "She would find herself married to a rum barrel."

"He is a kindly man, sober, and patient and brave," said Nancy. "I think a wife could change him. He gave me two knitting needles of sperm whalebone that he made himself and told me he was a month working on each of them. I made him a stocking cap of red wool in return," she added simply.

"You care of him, daughter?" asked Peace of God.

She put down the quilt she was working on and looked at her father. "I do not know," she said. "I grow older and he is kind to me. And there is no one else. . . ." She got up suddenly from the chair and rushed to her room, leaving her father staring after her. "Lord," he said at length, "here's a turn of the wind I had not looked for. It was only yesterday she was playing with seashells and begging to be taken out to bring in the lobster pots."

At that moment there was a knock on the door, a heavy purposeful rap readily heard above the gusts of wind. Peace of God pulled back the bolt, stared, and then cried, "Peter Treegate!" The frontiersman entered, stooping under the lintel of the door. He seemed to fill the little parlor and utterly dwarfed Peace of God who motioned him to a chair beside the fire.

"You have become like Samson," said Peace of God wondering. "You have grown a foot since I last saw you at Saratoga and in the bloody days before that when the Maclaren of Spey went to his death in pride and stubbornness. God rest his soul, poor sinner that he was."

"He would curse you for a canting whiggish Sassenach if he heard you say that," said Peter, smiling.

"He would," said Peace of God without resentment. "But he was a good fighting man though as vain as a child. But what are you doing here? I thought you were in the Carolinas with General Gates."

"I came north for help and return tomorrow," said Peter. "I wanted to see you before I went away again."

"You can stay the night?"

"If you have room."

"I have only my daughter here. You can sleep before the fire and welcome. We have slept many a time in worse places."

"Then I'll gladly stay."

"You have not met my daughter," said Peace of God. "I will call her." He crossed to the door leading from the parlor which served also as a kitchen, into his daughter's bedroom, knocked on it and said, "Nancy. My friend Peter Treegate of whom I have spoken to you has called to see us."

She was a few minutes coming out and then stood hesitating in the door of her room, looking at a man who appeared to her so wild that she believed him an Indian. She was indeed afraid and came only hesitatingly into the room and dropped him a curtsey. He bowed and reached out his hand.

"We are old friends, your father and I," he said. Then he turned to Peace of God. "I had thought your daughter a child from the way you spoke of her."

"It is a mistake of fathers to think of their daughters so, sir," she said and then blushed on her own boldness.

"Captain Treegate will be staying for dinner and spend the night under our roof," said Peace of God. He needed to say nothing further. Nancy went to a small table close to which there was a sink fed with water from a barrel overhead, and she busied herself peeling potatoes and cutting meat for a stew. But every now and again she stole a glance at Peter Treegate and listened to the talk of war and the Carolinas and the hope of reviving the war in the South.

She had to come between the two men to put the pot of stew on the big hook over the fire. It was a big pot and required the strength of both her hands to lift it. As she was doing so Peter reached out and with one hand took the pot from her and put it easily on the hook. She shivered when her hand touched his. Then she took the quilt she had been working on, and returning to her chair, started stitching again. Peter looked at her.

"You work neatly," he said.

"She is as good with a sail as she is with a quilt," said Peace of God. "And she is neat with nets too, particularly the trammels. Trammels, you know, are three nets together, the fine mesh in the center and the two wider mesh on each side, to make a pocket in which to catch fish. But her skill is from God and she must take no pride in it for without His hand nothing can be done on earth."

"Would you say," said Peter smiling, "that God steered your hand when you threw your Bible in the face of the English gunner at Trenton?"

"I would," said Peace of God gravely. "It would be sinful pride to think my aim was sure only because of myself." Then he added with rare humor, "It was a good thing it was the full text and not just the four Gospels, for there was plenty of heft to it. But I sit here in idle talk, though with a friend," he continued, "when there is a poor soul trembling on the brink of hell at this moment and I must snatch him to safety."

"Who's that?" asked Peter.

"Simmons, my master gunner," replied Peace of God. "He cannot stay away from spirits and, with the storm raging, I have no doubt he is in the Blue Anchor at the moment tossing back pots of rum. I must get him out of there and back aboard the *Defiance*. If he is not sober when the wind dies and we weigh anchor, he will be useless for three days."

"Shall I come with you?" asked Peter thinking the little fisherman might have a hard time getting a master gunner out of a taproom.

"Nay," said Peace of God. "Daughter, reach me the new pamphlet containing John Wesley's thoughts on the drinking of gin and other devilish waters. That will be enough." Nancy went to a chest of drawers, pulled a drawer open and returned with a much thumbed pamphlet which she gave to her father. "Do not be hard on him," she said gently.

"I will be all brotherly love and kindness, sweet as honey," said Peace of God calmly, "though it is possible I will have to break his head. But that is nothing if I can save his soul." With that he flung a seacloak over his shoulder, said he would be back within the hour, and went out into the storm headed for the Blue Anchor Inn by the waterfront.

"Your father is one of the strangest men I have ever met," said Peter when they were alone. "At times he is like some prophet out of the Bible, roaring about righteousness and calling on all to repent. And yet I have

seen him as gentle as a woman when someone is hurt.
Aye, and seen him weep when someone died."

"He has spoken often of you," said Nancy, "and prays
for you every night."

"Prays for me?" cried Peter. "Why?"

"Because of your upbringing, which he says was
among men of pride and blood and because of your
strength, which he fears may be your downfall. And also
because of your own pride which he says must be humbled if you are to be saved. He calls you Young Samson
in his prayers."

"And how does he pray?" asked Peter.

"He says 'Lord, in Your infinite mercy, remember our
young Samson, Peter Treegate, raised among the fierce
Scots in the wilderness and taught, when little more
than a babe, many superstitions and vain beliefs. Strike
him down, Lord, that he may be saved to everlasting
joy and glory. But Lord, do not hurt him too much.
Amen.'"

"I'd sooner he offered such prayers for my enemies
than for me," said Peter, not entirely pleased. "I think
he misjudges me on the subject of pride."

Nancy shook her head. "You are too big and strong
and young not to be proud of your strength," she said.
"And that is sinful. And you have been brought up on
bloody deeds and are a man of blood, and that is not
pleasing to the Lord."

"What else is a man to do in time of war?" asked
Peter, nettled that this girl whom he had just met should
hold such an opinion of him.

"Nothing, in time of war, Captain Treegate," she said

quietly. "But have your thoughts ever turned to peace and what you are to do then?"

"Why," said Peter, "when peace comes, if I live, I'll settle down and re-establish my father's business in Boston. There may be no Crown, but there will still be trade and shipping."

Nancy looked calmly at his wild but handsome face. The skin was as brown as leather, but there was a wide white scar which stretched from the left cheekbone to the neck below his ear. That, she knew, was from a bullet wound received at the battle of Princeton. She also knew that his right shoulder had been smashed by a musket ball in the same battle. Her father had told her all these things.

"You will look strange in Boston in your deerskins," she said quietly. "And stranger still clad in homespun and sitting at a counting desk, Captain Treegate. I think you would rather be among wild bears and Indians than the citizens of Boston."

He was surprised that so much insight should be possessed by so mild a girl whose life had been completely protected from the world around.

"What of yourself?" he said. "What lies ahead in your future?"

"I hope to marry," she said with no more emotion than if she were announcing that she hoped to cook dinner.

"And have you some fortunate fellow in mind?" asked Peter. She raised her head from her quilting and looked at him steadily and he felt under that look that she had known him for many years.

"I will marry whom God sends me as my spouse," she said.

"And how will you know who he is?" asked Peter.

"When God sends someone," she replied, "there is no room for doubt."

"I trust you will be happy with him then," said Peter.

She smiled. "That would not matter," she said. "It is more to the point that I would be but half alive without him."

Meanwhile Peace of God Manly had arrived at the taproom of the Blue Anchor to find it, as he said later, "filled with smoke like the waiting room of hell." There were several men at tables playing cards and others roaring a chorus of "The Derby Ram" with Master Gunner Simmons, his back to the mantelpiece and a tankard in his big fist, beating out the time and playing the part of shantyman.

"That ram and I got tiddely, sir; as tiddely as could be," roared Simmons. "And when we sobered up, sir; we was far away to sea."

"Silence, sinners all," shouted Peace of God, slamming the taproom door shut to such effect that the glasses rattled on the tables, and Simmons, who had opened his huge mouth to get a good start on the chorus, was left gaping and utterly bewildered at what seemed to him the miraculous appearance of his captain in the taproom.

All in the room turned to look at Peace of God, and one of the cardplayers flung his hand down on the table and muttered something about an ill wind and holding three aces.

"Thou should'st be in thy church at this moment, Master Sexton," cried Peace of God, shaking a bony finger at this player. "Seeing all is seemly for tomorrow's services at which I will preach on gaming and licentiousness which two vices brought about the fall of Jericho. And you," turning to another of the players, "did I not lend thee two shillings yesterday to feed thy children only to find thee throwing away their food at a card table.

"Ah, poor weak mortals all. See how what you think is joy reaps nothing but misery; your children hungry and your wives, patient as lambs, anxiously awaiting you in their homes."

"Lamb isn't the word I'd choose for my Sarah," said one of the cardplayers. "Not when she reaches for the fire iron as I come through the door."

"The more shame on you that you should turn her from lamb to lion by your own behavior," cried Peace of God. "I remember Sarah when she was a child and mild as a May morning. And you, Master Gunner," turning on Simmons, "why art thou not aboard the *Defiance* as ordered?"

"I thought to come here, so help me, Cap'n," said Simmons, "and spread the word of the Lord among these ungodly folk as you are doing now." There was a guffaw from the others but Peace of God paid no attention to it.

"And you have fallen into the same pit as you trusted to rescue these others from," he said. "Come back aboard with me now, Master Gunner, and we will go down on our knees together and pray that the Lord will let the grace of salvation at last pour into your soul."

"No," said Simmons suddenly desperate. "Not I, Captain. I can weather the shakes that come on me after a bout of drinking, but praying on top of it is more than mortal man can abide. I'll stay here. No man will make me budge."

"Come, Master Simmons," said Peace of God moving slowly towards him.

Simmons looked around for an avenue of escape but there was only one door in the taproom, and Peace of God stood between him and that door.

"Don't lay a hand on me, Captain," he said. "Don't lay a hand on me for by thunder I'll stretch you out on the floor." But Peace of God moved steadily forward, looking very mild. Simmons lunged at him but Peace of God slipped below the blow, put his head down, and charging like a goat, butted Simmons in the stomach. The gunner went to the floor without a sound.

"Like Paul," said Peace of God looking at him, " 'tis hard for thee to kick against the goad." Then he hauled the winded gunner to a sitting position, and with remarkable strength, put him on his shoulder and carried him out.

"I'd sooner have a wife like Sarah than a captain like Peace of God," said the one who had spoken earlier. "Between Scripture and the Articles of War, a man wouldn't have a chance serving under him."

*3* ☆

The Carolinas are a land of rivers, bounded in the north by the Dan which in its lower reaches becomes the Roanoke and in the south by the Savannah. Between these two broad streams is a network of waterways, flowing all from the mountains in the northwest to the ocean in the east. Peedee, Wateree, Enoree, Congores, Santee, Combathee—for the greater part their names are those given them by the Indians. These rivers in the mountains flow through gulches and valleys and boulder-strewn forests which rise steeply from the river bed as if to mount to the sky. Approaching the coastal areas many of them wander through fetid marshlands full of wild fowl and sawgrass, mudflats, quicksands and ancient oaks draped with gloomy shrouds of Spanish moss.

This country Peter Treegate knew well, for he had been brought up in the highlands of the Carolinas. He was glad to be back in them. He had ridden through the New England states to the Dan River, which forms in places the southern border of Virginia, and then knowing the country ahead, left his horse. He now struck out on foot along the foothills of the Appalachians. He had come twenty miles on foot that day through a drowning rain and was seeking a particular cave which lay at the bottom of a valley down which he was now heading. The sides of the valley were thick with pines which grew so close together in places that clumps of them had to be skirted. There were big boulders strewn here and there among the pines, some as large as houses and the red earth glittered under a sheet of water which cascaded in a thousand rivulets down the valley slopes to the river below.

The rain, coming through the branches of the pines, made a surprisingly loud hissing sound and the rivulets produced a tinkling noise, like someone playing on a spinet piano. But beyond these two sounds there was nothing to be heard for there was no wind with the rain. Peter himself moved noiselessly and easily down the valley, delighting despite the weather in the loneliness and wilderness of the area in which it seemed that no human being had ever set foot since the dawn of time. This was his homeland, the part of America which he felt belonged especially to him and he knew all the settlers in these wild areas and every mountain and valley and ridge which they contained. He was here on a task he had set himself—to raise a force of men among the mountaineers to fight the British. There would be many difficulties because of the feuds among the mountaineers, but he believed he would succeed.

Suddenly, above the hissing of the rain and the tinkling of the rivulets he heard from the bottom of the valley below him another sound. It was a faint shout, followed a second later by a report of a musket. He froze in his tracks and then, moving silently to a huge boulder nearby, whose top rose sixty feet above the sloping sides of the valley, climbed it as agile as a monkey and peered over the edge, squinting a little to be able to see the better through the white deluge of rain. Ahead, pines and rain obscured his view so he could not see to the floor of the valley from which the cry and the shot had come. But to the left and fifty yards below him was a precipice and over the top of this he could get a glimpse of the river below. He waited, watching this area, the white gleam of the river showing palely between the dark pines.

After a little while a horse and rider appeared. The horseman was dressed in bright green clothing and wore a coonskin cap. He was in view for only a second or two and then disappeared to be quickly followed by another and then another horseman. Peter counted twenty in all.

When the last of the riders, all of whom were armed, had gone by, Peter slipped down from the rock and moved swiftly down the valley to the place whence the shot had come. He found a man dragging himself along the ground from the side of the swift flowing river. One of his legs was all blood. The man looked up at Peter and his eyes were glazed with pain.

"I'm a friend," said Peter. "Don't be afraid."

"I thought you were one of Ferguson's men, come back to make a better job of me," said the other.

"Ferguson's men?" repeated Peter. Major Patrick Ferguson was well known in the southern colonies. A British officer, he had raised a force of Tories—Americans who opposed the revolution—and they had raided settlements and plantations all over South Carolina. Ferguson's men, together with Tarleton's dragoons, were the most feared of the British forces in the South. They gave no quarter, burning, pillaging and looting, and using the Revolution as a means to obtain private revenge. But Peter was surprised that they should be raiding so far into North Carolina.

"What are Ferguson's men doing so far north?" he asked.

"Raiding," said the other tersely. "The British plan to push into North Carolina and then Virginia. Ferguson goes ahead softening up the country for Cornwallis who will follow with the regulars."

Peter took his hunting knife and slit the man's breeches to examine his wound. "I seem to know you," he said. "Where are you from?"

"Fraserville, five miles up the river."

Peter nodded. He knew the settlement.

"Who are you?" the man asked.

"Peter Treegate."

The other drew in his breath in surprise. "The Maclaren of Spey's foster son?" he said. Peter nodded. "This is bad country for you, Peter Treegate," said the man. "The Farquesons have not forgotten the feud between themselves and the Maclaren. They've vowed to take your scalp and nail it to a tree."

"That is all forgotten as far as I am concerned," said Peter.

"You may have forgotten it, but the Farquesons haven't. I think the Farquesons were behind Ferguson's raid. They are Tories anyway and side with the Redcoats."

"You'll be the Red Fraser," said Peter remembering the man now. "You are lucky. The shot went through the muscle but the bone isn't broken. I'll have to take the bullet out or it will poison in two hours. Can you stand the pain?"

"I will have to," said the Red Fraser. "You haven't a dram of rum on you?"

"No," said Peter. He fished in his bullet bag and took out a slug. "Here," he said, giving it to the man, "chew on that. It will stop you biting your tongue."

He felt the edge of his hunting knife and, not finding it to his liking, stropped it quickly on the arm of his deerskin jacket. Then he turned the Red Fraser over on his face and drove the knife into his thigh and made a quick slicing cut. He felt the bullet under the edge of the blade, put the knife on the ground and reached with his fingers into the cut he had made. The Red Fraser screamed but in a moment Peter had the bullet between thumb and forefinger. He threw it on the ground in front of the man.

"Keep it to remember Ferguson by," he said. Then he cut a strip of deerskin from the end of his hunting shirt, about two inches wide, and used this to bandage up the Red Fraser's thigh.

"Stand up and see if you can walk," he said when he was through. The other rose gingerly, spitting out the bullet he had in his mouth. It was chewed as flat as a half dollar. "I can walk a piece," he said. "But not fast."

"Come on then," said Peter and led the way upstream.

Two hours later they had arrived at the settlement of Fraserville. All these settlements in the valleys of the Appalachians had been made by Scottish clans who had arrived there after the failure of the Scottish rising of 1745. But as Peter knew, the emigrants had brought their clan feuds and loyalties with them and still thought of themselves as Scottish Highlanders rather than Americans. It was his job to get them to see themselves as Americans and join in the war against the British. But the task, he realized, was going to be difficult, the more so since the old feud with the Farquesons in the neighboring valley was still alive.

Fraserville was nothing now but a heap of ashes and charred wood. Not a cabin was left standing and the women of the settlement stood about in the ruins, their children, white-faced with terror, clinging to their long skirts.

When they saw Peter enter the clearing in which the settlement stood, some of them fled but a few stood their ground. Then they recognized the Red Fraser and gathered around him, babbling questions so fast that he could not answer them.

"Are there any men left alive?" asked Peter when he could get attention. The woman he put this question to, aged and white haired, looked at him suspiciously.

"Who asks the question?" she said.

"Peter Treegate that was the foster son of the Maclaren of Spey," he replied.

"What are you doing here?" she asked still suspicious.

"I am here to get men to fight the British and I am going to make my peace with the Farquesons and get their aid," Peter replied.

"All you will get from the Farquesons will be a smile to your face and a knife to your back," said the woman.

"You have not answered my question," said Peter. "Are there any men of the Frasers left besides the Red Fraser here?"

"There are two," said the woman sullenly. "Colin son of Colin and the Yellow Head. Colin son of Colin has gone to get the Magraws and the Yellow Head the Campbells to revenge the raid."

"Good," said Peter. "Then I will get the Farquesons."

"You will not move from this place," said the Red Fraser grimly. "The Farquesons are our enemies and have brought this on us."

"They will always be your enemies if you blame everything that happens on them," said Peter. "I will go to them and tell them that I need men to fight the British—frontiersmen and riflemen. I think I will bring some back."

"They have sworn to lift your scalp as I told you before and they will kill you," said the Red Fraser.

"If I were a woman I might believe that," said Peter. "But I am a man and will find out for myself." With that he turned on his heel and headed out of the settlement.

The Farqueson settlement, larger than that of the Frasers, was in the neighboring valley four hours away. Peter had been walking since dawn of that day and it was now four in the afternoon and would be dark in an hour. Nonetheless he set out for he could, if needed, walk twenty-four hours resting only to eat. The rain had stopped and about seven the moon came from behind a bank of clouds, giving him all the light he needed. He reached the Farqueson settlement about ten-thirty and every dog in the place announced his coming.

He went straight to the cabin of Donald Farqueson, the head of the clan, and when he got to the door it was opened without his knocking. He knew from this that he had been watched through every window and peephole as he walked through the empty streets of the settlement in the moonlight. Donald Farqueson was sitting at a rough table with his three sons—Fergus, Ian and Donald Oge, who was the eldest. He was a big gaunt man, the flesh of his cheeks hanging down in furrows. He had a long thin nose, and his hair was white and came to his shoulders. There were two candles made of bear tallow burning on the table. The door had been opened by Brid Farqueson, the only daughter and she, at a sign from her father, went into the only other room the cabin possessed.

Peter, standing in the doorway, looked at the four

men sitting around the table. These were the men who had killed his foster father. They had done so to avenge the killing of one of their women by the Maclaren of Spey. Their faces were grim and their eyes like nail-heads. He took off his rifle which was slung muzzle down over his shoulder and stood it outside the door. Then he pulled out his hunting knife and threw it on the table so that it slithered in the silence towards Donald Farqueson. It was the token that he had come in peace. Ian Farqueson let the corner of his thin mouth curl up in a smirk of contempt but the others showed no emotion.

"Bring a stool for the Maclaren's son," said Donald Farqueson at last, but without turning his head from Peter. The girl Brid appeared from the other room and set a stool at the end of the table, facing her father.

Peter glanced at the girl. Her hair was red and came down to her waist. She had a lovely face and there was a suggestion of a smile in her eyes, but seeing him looking at her, she lowered her head and blushed. When she had gone Peter sat on the stool and Donald Farqueson said, "Why are you here among your blood enemies?"

"You have my knife," said Peter. "I come in peace."

"You will not be harmed then for twenty-four hours," said the Farqueson. "But we have vowed to kill you."

"I have heard of it," said Peter. "Why?"

"Because your foster father killed one of our women and her child."

"My foster father is dead," said Peter. "You have had your revenge."

"He is dead but you are alive," said Ian Farqueson. "The Maclaren killed two Farquesons, one a bairn—no more than a wee child."

"I had no hand in it," said Peter. "I disowned the Maclaren when I heard of it."

"Because you were afraid," said Ian Farqueson with a sneer.

"Because I thought he did wrong," said Peter quietly.

"Because you were afraid," insisted Ian.

Peter looked at him calmly. "I have given you my reason," he said. "As for my courage, there are others who are in a better position to judge of it." Then he turned to Donald Farqueson.

"Ferguson's men raided the Frasers today and killed all but three of their men. It is said that the Farquesons had a hand in the raid."

"We don't need Redcoats to settle our quarrels," growled the other.

"Did you have any hand in it?" Peter insisted.

"No," said Farqueson. "I did not. Nor did anybody from here. You say all but three of the men were killed?"

"Yes."

"The Big Fraser was among those killed?"

"He was," said Peter. "Those who lived were Colin son of Colin, the Yellow Head, and the Red Fraser."

"God rest his soul then," said Donald Farqueson. "He was a blood enemy but a brave man. I am sorry that the Redcoats killed him. He fought well in the Forty-five. I would have wished him peace in his old age." He got up and went to a makeshift cupboard and returned with four mugs and a bottle. He gave each of his sons a mug and poured some spirits from the bottle into them and said, "We should drink to a good journey for the Big Fraser now that he is on the dark side of life." Then they drank the toast.

Peter had not been included in it, but took no affront. This was an affair between the Farquesons and the Frasers and no concern of his. When the toast had been drunk Donald Farqueson said, "Tell the Frasers when you get back that we drank godspeed to their chief." Then he added, "They will know then that we had no hand in the raid."

"I am hoping that some of the Farquesons will go back with me to Fraserville," said Peter. "I am going to raise a body of men to fight against the Redcoats in the war."

"The war is no concern of ours," growled Donald Farqueson. "And anyway there is a quarrel between you and Ian."

"There is no quarrel as far as I am concerned," said Peter. "I came in peace, to ask for two things—first an end to the feuding between the clans at least until this war is over, and second that the Farquesons send some men to join the Magraws and the Campbells and the Robertsons and fight against the Redcoats."

"Under whose command?" asked Donald Farqueson.

"Mine," said Peter.

"Who would fight under a coward?" sneered Ian Farqueson.

Donald Farqueson half rose from his stool and hit his son Ian such a blow as to knock him to the floor.

"You have three times under my roof put the name coward on this man who is my guest," he said. "And you do yourself no credit calling a man a coward who under the laws of hospitality cannot defend himself. Now hear what I have to say, Ian, and you too Fergus and Donald Oge. I have known this man since he was a boy and he is no coward. If he were a coward, he would not have come here among his enemies. And if he were a coward, he would not have fought in the war in the northern colonies. So I say he is no coward and I will not have that name put on him.

"I will grant you that he has not a proper sense of honor for he is not truly of the Highlands. He was not brought up entirely among gentlemen, but spent part of his life in Boston which is full of merchants and people who have no sense of honor. These are people who go to court if an offense has been done them, instead of settling the matter themselves as any gentleman would. But he is not to be blamed for that.

"Although he is no gentleman then, he is not to be called a coward in my house. What is said to him outside is another matter."

The three sons of Donald Farqueson listened to this in silence but Ian was still sneering and Peter could tell that this man hated him deeply and would kill him if he had a chance. He was angry against Ian Farqueson, but fought against the anger because he could not afford to open an old feud. The cause he fought in now was bigger than any private feud or quarrel and he must get as many men as he could among the mountaineers to take up arms against the British and raiders like Ferguson. To reopen old feuds would be disastrous. He turned to Donald Farqueson.

"You are the leader of the men in this valley," he said. "You can put an end to the feuds in the mountains if you will say the word. It would be right to do so at least until this war is over."

"For what reason should they be put aside?" demanded Donald Farqueson. "It is not the part of a gentleman nor the son of a gentleman to forget a blood quarrel."

"The war is your war," said Peter.

"It is not our war at all," said Donald Farqueson. "It is the war of those merchants in Boston and it is fought for their profit and for nothing else. It does not concern us here in the mountains."

"It was not the Frasers' war then either," said Peter. "They took no hand in it. Yet the British raided their settlement and killed all the men but three. And they burned the settlement to the ground."

"I am sorry about the Frasers," said Farqueson, "but that has not happened to us."

"Not yet," said Peter. "But the British are planning to invade North Carolina. Do you think they will leave you alone here?"

"This is nothing that can be decided here and now," said Donald Farqueson. "I will sleep on it and you can talk to the men of the settlement in the morning. They have no love for you," he added grimly.

"I don't ask them to love me," said Peter. "I ask them only to decide which side they are on, for they must be on one side or the other."

"I will tell you what side I am on," said Ian Farqueson. "I am on whatever side is opposed to you, for I will kill you one day because of the killing of my wife and child."

Donald Farqueson picked up Peter's hunting knife which still lay on the table and tossed it to him. "You have not eaten all day, I would venture," he said. "Brid, bring food for our guest."

While Peter was eating, Ian Farqueson put on his powder horn, hunting knife, and bullet pouch and took his rifle from its bracket over the fireplace. He went out without a word and the others watched him go but said nothing.

*4* ☆

Peter was up before dawn the following morning and leaving the cabin went to draw water from the well at the back in which to wash himself. There was a ring of frost about, lying on the tips of the pines and the eaves of the cabins and on the rim of the bucket which he lowered by a rope into the well. His breath hung white in the clean sharp air and he stood for a moment luxuriating in the wonder of the new day which was so fresh and clear that it might have been the first day the world had ever known.

The sun was not yet up. What lighted the sky and the world around was the promise of its coming—a pale ghostly light which cast a kind of halo round the cabins of the settlement and the topmost pines that stood on the ridge of the mountainsides around. He heard the brisk chattering of squirrels and then the mournful piping of a blackbird and far away up the valley the howl of a timber wolf, the final salute of his night of hunting. Then all was silent for a moment, for the wolf's howl put a fright on all the forest creatures. Then the squirrels started their impudent chattering again and Peter grinned and lowered the wooden bucket into the well and drew it up filled with freezing spring water.

He stripped to the waist, splashed the water over his face and arms and chest and then, taking a deep breath, plunged his head into the bucket and came up with water streaming from his long dark hair. When he opened his eyes, Brid Farqueson was standing before him holding a cloth. He took it and rubbed himself briskly while she looked at him gravely.

"You are a big man, Peter Treegate," she said. She spoke simply, like a child. "I think you are the biggest man in these parts now except for Thomas McClintock who is bigger. It is a pity that you have no kinsmen behind you to be their chief."

"I have kinsmen," said Peter. "Thousands of them. The men of the Continental Army are all kin to me, for we fight in the same cause."

"They are not kinsmen," she scoffed. "There is no blood tie to them."

"There are stronger things than blood ties," said Peter patiently. "There are ideas that men have in common and they work together to attain or fight side by side to achieve them. Out of blood ties come clans. Out of ideas come nations. Nations are bigger than clans."

She considered this while he put on his shirt of deer-skin. Then she left without a word and went back to the cabin. He now spilled some water over his feet to wash them and, when they were dried, returned to the cabin. He found the girl Brid mending a rent in the moccasins. The Farqueson men were up and Donald Farqueson looked sourly at his daughter and said, "Your brothers need your attention. Why do you work on this man's moccasins?"

She looked steadily at her father and said, "He is our guest." Donald Oge laughed and rumpled her long red hair, and she blushed and went on with her work. Their breakfast consisted of a mush made of parched corn and some cold venison, washed down with spring water. While they were eating, the men of the settle-ment gathered outside the Farqueson cabin and stood around in silence. There were perhaps thirty of them and Peter went out to talk to them. They all had their weapons with them and looked at him in stony silence.

"Most of you here know me or have heard of me," said Peter, "for I was brought up in these mountains. You look on me as an enemy because my foster father, the Maclaren of Spey, killed the wife and child of Ian Farqueson. I honored the Maclaren of Spey, but I disowned him for that deed, as you know. But the score is settled for he himself was killed as you know and it is not on this business that I am here now."

The men continued to stare at him in silence.

"You have heard that the Tories under Major Ferguson raided the Frasers yesterday," he continued. "The war which you thought was far away is here now and you must choose your sides. The Magraws and Campbells are meeting over in the Fraser's valley. I am here to get men from the Farquesons to join and fight the British. If any of you wish to volunteer, let him step forward. He will serve as a soldier in the Continental Army and in the service of the Continental Congress."

A little bearded man, so small that his rifle seemed taller than he, ignoring Peter, said to Donald Farqueson, "What is your opinion about this war? Does it concern us at all?"

"It does not concern the older men," said Donald Farqueson. "We had our war and we lost it in Scotland in the rising of Forty-five and came here to start our lives again. But I am beginning to think that this war concerns the younger men, for this is the country they were born in and they should take a hand in its wars."

"And why should the younger men fight in it?" asked the little man. "We have taken no part in it up to now and I do not care for myself who wins it. But if we take a part now, the Redcoats will send their troopers up here and burn the settlement as they did with the Frasers'." He looked directly at Peter. "It is all right for you. You have no clan and no kin. But it is different for us."

Peter felt his temper mounting. He was tired of this talk of kin and clans; tired of the narrow viewpoints of these mountain men who looked on their own valleys as the beginning and the end of the world.

"You say I have no clan and no kin and in the sense you use the words that is true," he said. "But there was a Boston apprentice killed by my side at Breed's Hill and he is kin to me for I was in the same battle. And there was a farmer died of cold when I was carrying him on my back in the raid of Princeton and he is kin to me also though I do not know his name. And there are good men dead by bayonets or bullets or hanging from Quebec to Savannah and they are all kin to me and part of my clan for they died in the cause that is my cause and your cause. And that cause is liberty.

"But make no mistake about it. I want only men with me who will fight for the cause of the whole country. If any of you come, come on those terms or stay here. But I will tell you this; there are farmers in New England that you would think of as servants, who have given their lives and their son's lives in this cause. They have fought battles against odds that would make you quail, and they have done this for you, though you do not know it. They are fighting now while you stand around like women arguing the fine points of the situation. And if the Redcoats do not come up into these valleys and you are left undisturbed here, you can thank these same New England farmers and shop-keepers and merchants for it, though you would not pass the time of day with them were you to meet them here, thinking them too lowly born."

With that he moved down into the crowd only to find his way blocked by one of the men as big as himself who put his hands on his hips and said, "I have a mind to break your neck for saying that the New England farmers are better than we."

The others moved away leaving the two in a little circle. Peter looked around at them and now they were smiling for this man was Thomas McClintock, a cousin of the Farquesons, and the best fighter in the valley. Peter saw Brid among the crowd looking very innocent and he wondered whether it was she who had summoned McClintock. "Let me pass," he said.

"Not without a fight," said McClintock. Peter shrugged.

"Do you want to wrestle or do you want to use the knife?" he asked. At the word "knife" there was a little gasp of excitement from the crowd.

McClintock passed the tip of his tongue around his lips and then grinned. "The knife would make it more pleasurable," he said. "But perhaps you have no stomach for it."

For answer Peter drew his hunting knife and stuck it up to the hilt in the ground in the center of the little clearing in which they were standing. McClintock gave his to another to hold for him, and the two backed off to the edge of the circle, facing each other. McClintock crouched to the ground, ready to spring to the center at the signal and get the knife. This was the way these matters were handled; one knife between two men, and whoever got it had the other at his mercy. Peter, however, did not crouch. He remained standing at the edge of the circle.

"Let the Farqueson give the signal," said McClintock.

The Farqueson looked at the two men, frowning in puzzlement to see that Peter was not crouched to spring into the center of the circle to get the hunting knife before McClintock.

"Are you ready?" he asked.

"Yes," said McClintock.

"Yes," said Peter.

"Go," cried the Farqueson.

McClintock lunged across the area to the knife, giving at the end of the lunge a spring which carried him to it. He grabbed the hilt of the knife with a cry of delight and was rising with it when Peter aimed a kick at his arm which knocked McClintock backward, though he still held the knife.

McClintock was on his feet in a second and, roaring like a bull, charged at Peter. Peter grabbed McClintock's arm and twisting quickly hurled him to the ground. The knife flew several feet away. McClintock, who had hit the ground with his back, lay there for a moment, winded. Peter walked over, picked up the knife and threw it to McClintock. There was a low murmur from the spectators.

"Come on," Peter said. "I am hardly warmed by the exercise."

McClintock, in a black rage, charged him again, giving a roar of fury. Peter flung himself toward McClintock and struck him a blow on the shoulder that could be heard on the outskirts of the crowd. The blow was so heavy that McClintock was turned sideways by it. But he swung his knife arm in an arc and when he raised the knife again the blade was red. Peter staggered away from him, the blood flowing from a wound on his neck.

McClintock lunged again and Peter grabbed his wrist and the two wrestled in the center of the clearing for possession of the knife. McClintock had the advantage, pressing Peter's arm back so that the blade of the knife came nearer and nearer to his throat. The muscles of the men's arms and shoulder showed beneath their deerskins. Their breath came in gasps which were like little sharp cries. The veins on McClintock's face and neck were standing out under the strain and his eyes were full of fury.

The knife crept by centimeters towards Peter's throat until it seemed to some in the crowd that the point must be touching his skin. But McClintock seemed incapable of driving the blade any further for it stayed there without moving. Then, as if he had hardly been using any strength at all up to this time, Peter pushed McClintock's hands away from him and twisted the other's wrists. McClintock dropped the knife, his face screwed up with pain. Peter heaved him away so hard that he stumbled backward and fell to the ground. Then Peter picked up the knife once more. McClintock started to back away, looking anxiously around for a place to escape for he thought he was to be killed. But Peter threw the knife to him once more.

"Try again," he said. "I begin to enjoy the sport."

The knife fell at McClintock's feet. He crouched

slowly to get it, not taking his eyes off Peter. All eyes were on the big mountaineer. He got the knife in his hand, then he stood up slowly, leaving the knife on the ground.

"I have had my fill," he said. "You are a better man than I am, Peter Treegate."

Peter walked over to him and held out his hand. "You are a good fighting man," he said. "I would like you to come with me, Thomas McClintock. But if you come, come as a soldier of the Continental Army and not as a member of the Farqueson clan."

One of the women in the crowd, for there were many of them present, came to Peter and made him sit on the steps of the Farqueson cabin while she examined the cut in his neck. It was perhaps a quarter of an inch deep, but no major blood vessels had been severed, though it was bleeding copiously. She got some ashes from the fire in the Farqueson cabin and when they were cool put them on the wound to staunch the bleeding. Then she bound Peter's neck with a cloth bandage and he thanked her.

"You need have no fear of steel nor of water," she said. "But be careful of the rope, Peter Treegate.

"Yes," said the woman, "the hangman's rope. There is a mark on your neck and it is the mark people have who are to be hanged."

"There are many who would like to hang me," said Peter, "but they must first catch me."

With that he retrieved his knife, picked up his rifle and powder horn and bullet bag and without a further word, started out of the settlement back towards the

Fraser's valley. He climbed the side of the separating mountain and turned when he was halfway up its flank. Then he saw, below him, a string of men following with McClintock in the lead. He counted twelve, turned, and went on.

*5* ☆

The total force Peter Treegate led out of the Appalachian mountains to war was thirty-seven men. There were Farquesons and Robertsons and McDonalds and McClintocks and Campbells and McNeils and McGillivrays. They sprawled behind him in groups of two or three, each man staying with his kinfolk for what marched behind Peter was not merely thirty-seven expert riflemen, each with his own Deckhard muzzle loader, but a dozen feuds reaching back through the centuries though put aside, by common consent, for the moment. Still the men stayed with their own folk. It would be Peter's job to break down the distrust of centuries which lay between one family and another, and make them into soldiers fighting in a common cause.

They were headed for Sycamore Flats on the Catawba River, for Peter had received news that this was the gathering place of an army of men who had come together to resist the British invasion of North Carolina. They arrived in three days from Fraserville, covering in that time a distance of a hundred and ten miles.

They found nearly a thousand men camped on the flats, living in shelters made of the branches of trees, or of tarpaulins propped up on a pole to give a rough resemblance of a tent. A more mixed company of men—they could not be called an army—would be hard to imagine. Some, like Peter's, were from the mountains and wore the mountaineer's deerskins. Some were small farmers from the foothills and the lowlands who wore broad-brimmed hats of felt and rough clothes of homespun. Their stockings were in tatters and many of them were barelegged and had sacking on their feet instead of shoes. For weapons they had scythes and pitchforks and occasionally a musket or a fowling piece. Others again were merchants from Charleston and Camden dressed in good clothes which were now however much soiled with the weather. These carried small swords by their sides which looked incongruous in the wilderness and several had pistols tucked in their belts. Others yet were wealthy planters, with a touch of the aristocrat to them, though their plantations had been burned by the Tories and their families had had to flee north to Virginia or some other place of safety.

All of them however had this in common—a burning hatred of the invaders. It was indeed more than a hatred. It was a fierce anger, for they had seen unarmed men shot or hung, and fields of crops, of tobacco or cotton or buckwheat, needlessly burned. They had seen homes set fire, wells polluted and dams blown up and in all of this there was a senselessness that had aroused them to the point where they could stand by no longer, idle spectators of a war about which they had not been previously concerned.

Some of the men at Sycamore Flats had earlier sided with the British and denounced as ungrateful rebels those of their neighbors who had taken up arms in the Continental cause. But now they cursed the very name of the King and, remembering how a fair countryside had been turned into a wilderness, swore that they would not go home until they had had their vengeance.

But though they had a common cause, they had not a common leader. They had gathered here on hearing of Ferguson's raid into North Carolina. Their purpose was to fall on him and destroy his force. But Peter soon found that the thousand men were all divided between half a dozen leaders. And none of these leaders could agree to set one of themselves in overall command.

"We've been here close to a week," a Camden tavern keeper said to Peter. "Four days and not a decision made. I tell you sir, we will fight. But by thunder the worst part of it is to find one man to lead us."

"Best talk to Nollichucky Jack," said a rifleman from the foothills of the Blue Ridge mountains. "Wily as a fox is Nollichucky. He knows more than anybody."

"Is he here?" cried Peter, delighted, for he knew Nollichucky Jack well.

"He is," said the other. "Over by the forge looking

after the blacksmithing." And with that he went on with whittling a plug of wood to provide a stopper for his water bag which was made of a goat's stomach.

Peter went over to a forge at the far end of Sycamore Flats, to find Nollichucky Jack, his hands on his hips, watching a number of horses being shod. He was a man of medium height with a very red face and dark hair which came down to his shoulders. He was probably the best dressed man in the whole assembly, having on a fine coat of light blue over a pair of excellent white breeches.

"Nollichucky!" cried Peter. "Where did you get that coat?"

"Treegate!" cried the other. "Well, here's a miracle at last! By thunder I begin to feel better about the whole situation right now. Where have you been? I lost sight of you at the rout at Camden and thought you were taken prisoner."

"Not me," said Peter. "I saw de Kalb cut down when the Redcoats broke through, but I escaped to the hills. A few of us rallied there and did some raiding and then I talked with Marion and went north to ask for help." He drew Nollichucky aside out of earshot of the others.

"We may get a replacement for Gates," he said. "A man who will co-operate with the partisans and put some spirit back into the regulars. That's what I asked for and I didn't make any bones about it."

"And who did you ask?" demanded Nollichucky. "Some foppish aide de camp that's never seen a shot fired in anger?"

"No. General Washington."

"Washington?" cried the other. "You got to see him?"

"Yes. He seemed to think that the issue would be decided with the recapture of New York. I told him plainly that if he lost the South he would have lost the war anyway. I asked for a replacement for Gates—for a fighting man instead of a pompous poser. I think we'll get one. But what's happening here?"

"Here?" cried Nollichucky. "Why here we have a modern Tower of Babel. To be sure, everybody speaks the same language but they all talk to a different purpose. To be short, we have six leaders instead of one. And having six leaders we have six plans. And six plans are as good as no plan. And so here we sit, with conferences every night and nothing decided."

"I've no mind to hang around here then," said Peter. "I've brought thirty-seven men out of the mountains and they've come to fight. Two days here and they will be going back again. Ferguson sent a party of Tories up to Fraserville and wiped out the settlement. My men want vengeance."

"Ferguson's headed south now," said Nollichucky. "He's trying to join up with Cornwallis. He has about eight hundred men with him; maybe more. It's plain what we should do. We should strike south and west right now and get between him and Cornwallis. But by the time that is agreed, it will be too late." He looked slyly at Peter out of the corner of his eyes.

"Do your men have horses?" he asked.

"No," said Peter. "We travelled on foot."

Nollichucky nodded to the forge. "I've got every

rideable horse in North Carolina here," he said. "I can let you have horses—for a price."

"What price?" asked Peter.

"Take a hundred men—your own and some I'll send with you—catch up with Ferguson, raid his camp and keep pestering him. Slow him down and drive him east toward us if you can. Head him off from Cornwallis. Much can be won or lost on a single throw of the dice right now."

Peter considered the proposition for a while. A hundred men against eight hundred—perhaps more. The odds were long. But everyone of his men was an expert with a Deckhard.

"Where do you want me to drive him to?" he asked.

"East," said Nollichucky. "Toward King's Mountain."

"King's Mountain?" cried Peter. "Why if he got to King's Mountain, he would be as safe there as if he were with the British garrison in New York."

"So he will think," said Nollichucky. "So he will think. And so I believe he will head there if you can harass him. But once he gets to the top of that ridge he will be like a treed fox. It is flat on the top as you know and not a hundred feet up the sides. There's no water up there and no food. And we can surround him with close to two thousand men. No, my friend, if we can get Ferguson on top of King's Mountain, we have him as good as beat. What do you say?"

"Get me the horses," said Peter. "We'll ride in an hour."

He went back to his men whom he had left under

Donald Oge Farqueson and McClintock on the eastern side of Sycamore Flats. He told these two, whom he had chosen as his lieutenants, that they were to go immediately on a raid, and they passed the word around. The men were delighted at the prospect of being provided with horses and when the horses came they leaped on their backs and galloped them around the encampment, jumping over shelters and campfires and hallooing in their delight. Next to a good rifle the mountaineers loved horses, which they rode bareback with nothing more in the way of harness than a halter. Peter had trouble rounding the men up again. When he got them together he told each man to wrap the metal links of the bits in cloth so they would make no noise.

"No white horses," he said. "Black or brown but none white. I don't want any horses that can be seen in the dark. And muddy up the white foreheads."

At last they were ready and set out in single file from Sycamore Flats. Each man carried with him his rifle, powder horn, bag of bullets and a supply of parched corn. They had a blanket apiece which served them as a saddle, but rode without stirrups, slouched over their mounts, their legs dangling down on each side. They looked like so many scarecrows on horseback, hardly a match for the neatness of the British cavalry they would meet. But these men could outride the best cavalrymen in the world. And when it came to fighting, they fought dismounted leaving their horses in the rear.

There was one further range of hills to be crossed before they got to the level lands beyond. These hills were thickly covered with bushes—rhododendrons for the greater part. As Peter and his men mounted into the hills a heavy mist swallowed them, cutting them off from Sycamore Flats. After a little while the mist turned to a freezing rain and then to snow which fell in particles no bigger than a grain of sand. The breath of the horses came in a stream of white as they plodded slowly upwards and soon the snow was three inches deep on the ground, completely muffling the sound of the hooves.

"You are a man born to good luck," said Donald Oge. "We could move a thousand men over these hills in this snow and nobody would know about it. How many men are there under Ferguson?"

"Eight hundred. Maybe more. There are some cavalrymen and the rest will be on foot."

"Do they have any cannon?" asked Donald Oge. He was big like his father but had the simplicity of a child. "I have never seen a cannon," he added. "But my father saw them and charged them. I would like to see a cannon."

"I don't think they have any," said Peter. "They are too cumbersome to take on a raid into the mountains and there is no use for cannon except in a pitched battle in the open."

"That is a pity," said Donald Oge. "I would like to charge a cannon like my father did. He has told me of it often and said that some wavered and he did not. A man will often lie about his courage but in this I think my father told the truth and I would like to know whether I am as brave a man as he. Tell me have you ever seen a cannon fired?"

"I have," said Peter.

"And what is it like?"

"There is a noise like thunder," said Peter. "If you are near you can feel the blow of it in your stomach as if you had been hit. Then there is a big cloud of smoke that rolls slowly away and out of the smoke comes a jet of fire. You can see the ball go through the air if you are standing in the line of flight—that is before the cannon or behind it. It hisses like a hot iron put into water. The shot will go three miles."

"I will not go back to my home until I have seen one and perhaps captured one," said Donald. "If I captured one then I would be proud to go back to my father. There is some talk among the men about prisoners. They do not know whether to cut their throats or hold them for ransom. Though the Campbells will take none because of what was done to their friends, the Frasers."

"If any men surrender, they are to be spared," said Peter sternly. "There is to be no killing of prisoners. And there will be no ransom."

"You have a queer way of looking at war," said Donald Oge. "What is the use of taking prisoners if you cannot make a profit out of them? But in any case I do not think many will be taken. The friends of the Frasers will kill any of the Tories or Redcoats they can, whether they surrender or not, and now that you have said there will be no ransom, I do not know that the Farquesons will take any prisoners themselves. It seems to me a waste of time."

"Your brother Ian may be one of the men riding with Ferguson," said Peter, quietly. "I think that was where he went when he left. If he surrendered would you want to cut his throat?"

"That is a foolish way to speak," said Donald Oge. "Ian is a Farqueson and would not surrender. A Campbell might surrender because it is well known that there is Sassenach blood in the Campbells though I will say nothing of that at this time. But the Farquesons are Scots and they would not surrender."

"Would you kill your brother Ian if you met him in battle?" Peter insisted.

"I would," said Donald Oge. "And to tell you the truth I find your question is foolish but that is because of your upbringing. Ian has chosen his side and I have chosen mine and what is important is that neither of us disgrace the name of our family by any kind of cowardice. So if I met him in battle I would kill him, and that is what he would expect me to do. He would be ashamed if I spared him because he was my brother."

They went on in the driving, fine snow in silence. When they had been going for four hours they stopped to rest the horses. The men threw the blankets over their mounts so that they would not take a chill, but themselves lay in the snow and slept for an hour. Then, their deerskins coated with snow, they rode on again, tougher and more enduring than the animals that carried them.

## 6 ☆

The sleet and then fine snow of the night had changed
to a thin gray rain, driven before a blustering easterly
wind, by dawn. The rain came at times in a cloud
striking out of the leaden sky and reducing visibility to
a few yards and the ground underfoot was soon a lake
of mud in which the horses stumbled, sometimes slip-
ping and falling on their hindquarters. It was weather
neither for travel nor for battle. Precisely because this
was so, Peter was anxious to push on. He was sure that
somewhere on the trail ahead, Ferguson and his Tory
Army would have camped for the night and would not
likely take to the road in such conditions. Nor would
the British be on guard against an attack. The very

adversity of the weather then provided an opportunity for a successful raid on the enemy.

Yet there was the condition of the men and the horses to be considered. Riders and mounts were soaking wet. The men needed some hot food and the horses needed to be fed and rubbed down to get the chill out of them. Peter looked for a place out of the wind and rain to rest his men and finding a small valley between the foothills called on them to dismount and tend their horses and make breakfast.

Because they were accustomed to living in the open, the men soon had fires going where others would have been shivering over cold fare. Each of them, as a matter of course, had picked up some dry sticks before leaving Sycamore Flats and put them inside their shirts. They made shelters to get out of the rain by stretching a blanket by its four corners over four sticks stuck in the ground, lit the fires on the leeward edge of the blanket where the smoke would be blown clear and there was no danger of the blanket burning, and were soon squatted around in their shelters cooking the parched corn they had brought.

Those not cooking gathered handfuls of rough grass and rubbed down the horses which were then allowed to feed on the grasses around. Peter posted two men on the trail ahead and two on the back trail as pickets and, passing through his little camp, was pleased to see that every man had wrapped the pan of his rifle in a piece of cloth to keep it dry and had put a plug of wadding down the barrel to stop water entering that way and causing a misfire. They were old hands at survival in the open in this kind of weather. One man had brought along a pack of cards and while the corn cooked started a game, for the mountain people were inveterate gamblers.

Donald Oge brought Peter a pan containing some hot corn meal. While Peter ate this, Donald Oge squatted down beside him. "Two of the horses are lame," he said staring ahead of him into the rain as if he were talking to himself.

"Badly?" asked Peter.

"If they are worked for another day they will be of no use for two weeks," said Donald Oge.

"Whose horses?" Peter asked.

"The Robertsons," replied Donald Oge and then he added contemptuously, "there was never a Robertson could take care of a horse."

Peter got up to look at the horses. The horses had, by common consent, gathered together in the lee of a hill and the steam was rising from their backs. It was not hard to find the two that were lame. They had drawn to one side. One was resting its left rear leg and the other its left foreleg. Peter inspected the animals and shrugged. "They'll have to be ridden," he said. "But we should overtake Ferguson by noon. Then maybe we'll exchange them for some of his."

At that moment there was a shout from the pickets down the trail and one of them came riding back and galloped over to Peter. "There's a queer little fellow coming up the road with a pony and a cart," he said. "He'll be a spy but I think you might like to talk to him before we cut his throat."

"Bring him here," said Peter.

The man, when he was brought, proved a strange individual indeed. He wore a beaver hat which being much too big for him created the impression that he had put a tar barrel on his head. He was a small man, no taller than five feet six inches so that among the mountaineers he looked like a boy—a boy who had raided his parents' attic and put on such clothes as took his fancy, whether they suited him or not.

He had a brocaded coat on his shoulders of a fashion that had gone out forty years before. It was a size and a half too big for him, so that the cuffs of the sleeves hid the ends of his fingers. He wore a pale waistcoat under this and his trousers were of butternut homespun and were tucked into a pair of jackboots that reached up to his thighs.

He had with him a pony which, though small, was sleek and well fed and the pony pulled a cart which had stretched over it on hoops a canvas cover. On one side of this cover was written the words "Knowledge Frees All" and on the other "Continental College and Traveling Book Store—James P. Paddock, Prop."

"Who are you?" asked Peter, wondering that so strange a creature should turn up in the Carolina wilderness. For answer the little man, with a flamboyant gesture, pointed to that side of the cart which contained the wording "Continental College and Traveling Book Store."

"I, sir," he said, "am that same James P. Paddock whose name you see limned upon the side of my equipage. And yourself, sir? I have not the pleasure of your acquaintance."

"Peter Treegate."

The man pursed his lips at this as if he had been presented with a problem which, while not beyond his mental abilities, yet provided some difficulties.

"Treegate," he said slowly, as if tasting the word and trying to analyze its content. "Treegate. That would be a Saxon name from the southern part of England in its origins. There might, however, be a Celtic touch to it, for we know of the Celts that it was their custom to plant a tree by their gateways as a guardian spirit. Hence Treegate. The custom survives to this day, as you have perhaps noted in your travels in more civilized parts. Yes, sir. Saxon, I would say, with Celtic overtones. And coming from the south of England likely you are of a Boston family."

Peter was so surprised at this spate of unsought and unexpected information that for a moment he could think of nothing to say.

"What are you doing here?" he asked eventually.

"Why sir," replied the other, "I bring light into the wilderness—culture into the homes of the ignorant and unlettered. I am the first and only traveling university of this great continent, dispensing science, philosophy and the sublime art of poetry throughout the nation. In short sir, I lend and sell books and have every kind of book needed to engage the attention of the inquiring mind. Spellers sir, for those who are taking their first steps towards reading. Two shillings the copy. And a new and excellent poem by Goldsmith called 'The Traveller.'"

"I suspect that you are a Tory spy," said Peter grimly.

"A completely understandable suspicion sir," said the other. "And yet my loyalties are entirely with the Continental cause and in the cause of that freedom without which life is ignoble and unsupportable, my bookshop in Boston was burned sir—burned to the ground."

"Where are you from?" asked Peter.

"My last stopping place sir, was the fort of Ninety Six where I sold three copies of a speller to some Hessian soldiers who may, I fancy, when this lamentable war is over, settle in this country. At least they seemed anxious to become acquainted with the language."

"Did you run into Ferguson's men ahead of us?" Peter asked.

"I did," replied the bookseller "and sold a copy of 'The Traveller' to Major Ferguson himself. As nice a gentleman as I have met in many a month—although loyal to the King. We discussed the essays of Addison and Steele and agreed that Addison had the more delicate style. I inquired the news of Dr. Samuel Johnson . . ."

"Never mind about Dr. Samuel Johnson," said Peter. "How far ahead is Ferguson."

"Ten miles," said Mr. Paddock. "Camped in a small valley with pickets thrown out to the northward. A thousand men I would say, two hundred of them mounted. Arms in good condition, but men weary. The horses are to the south of the camp and guarded by ten dragoons."

"You have a good eye for detail," said Peter significantly. "How have you escaped hanging so long?"

"Why sir," said the other, "it would be a crime against civilization itself to hang such a man as I. A harmless man sir, a man devoted more to the pen than the sword, the book than the field of war. I can give you the exact placement of the English army at the field of Agincourt in 1415, but I must confess that I took to my heels at Breed's Hill for there is no disguising the fact that I am an arrant coward. I'm as bold as Alexander among my books, sir, but have not the courage of a mouse when faced with musketry. Yet a man must live with himself and I have learned to tolerate my own cowardice, and there is some virtue in that. Yet I will confess to you that there are times when I thoroughly despise myself and groan aloud at my weakness."

"Well," said Peter, "if you are so familiar with the strategy of the Battle of Agincourt, perhaps you can draw me a map showing how Ferguson's men are camped ahead of us now."

"With all my heart," said the other. He picked up a piece of twig and sketched on the ground the disposition of the British forces ahead. Peter studied the map for some time. The British encampment was well chosen, lying between two hills with an open area before it so that no approach by daylight would go undetected. Mr. Paddock's map showed the location of the pickets and even if they could be driven back, this could not be done without alerting the whole British force which would come immediately to the attack. The situation, as sketched by the bookseller, seemed hopeless. To raid so strong a position would be to invite a disastrous defeat.

"A puzzler indeed," said Mr. Paddock. "There is the strength of a literate man. Major Ferguson, as I have said—although loyal to the King—is a fine gentleman and a great reader of books. The result is an educated mind, well versed in the arts of war. And the result of that, as you see, is a position which is almost impregnable."

"Why do you say almost?" asked Peter.

"I am permitted a word of advice?" asked Mr. Paddock.

Peter nodded, curious.

"Well, sir," said the bookseller, "you will note that the horses are south of the encampment and there are, as I have said, ten men guarding them. Now horses have not much sense and ten men may be readily scattered by such a force as yours. If you raid there to the southward, skirting the British encampment by going around the other side of the hills, so as not to be seen, the horses will certainly stampede. The British will run out after them and can be engaged for two or three rounds after which your own men, being mounted, can withdraw, wearing the laurels of victory without the payment of any great price."

Donald Oge, who had been listening with deep suspicion to the verbose little bookseller in the strange attire, said, "Yon man is a prattling Tory. Let us put a bullet through him and be on our way."

"My good sir," said Mr. Paddock anxiously, "I beseech you, do not speak so lightly of taking the life of the only man for a thousand miles around who can recite The Iliad of Homer in the original glorious Greek."

"He'll be a spy," warned Donald Oge, as if this was to be deduced from the very fact that the bookseller was familiar with the classics. He reached for his rifle as if to load it in preparation for the execution and Mr. Paddock, now very much afraid, removed and replaced his large beaver hat in extreme agitation as if undecided whether it would be more dignified for a man of his culture, a bookseller by profession, to be shot with it on or off.

He turned to Peter much agitated. "Sir," he pleaded "in the name of letters save me." It was plain that he believed he would be killed and killed that very minute.

"Get the men together here," said Peter to Donald Oge and then turning to Mr. Paddock he added, "Whether you are a spy or not will be decided in the next hour when we reach Ferguson's camp. Your life will depend on whether you have been telling the truth."

"Thank you sir," said Mr. Paddock. "Thank you. Thank you." He went immediately to his pony and commenced patting and fondling it, all the time telling the pony that they were not to be shot at all but were to be spared to continue their work of spreading learning through the wilderness. "Her name is Aesop sir," said Mr. Paddock. "A fitting name, for like the immortal Greek teacher, she is also a slave—though well treated."

When Donald Oge had got the men together Peter explained to them briefly what he had learned.

"There are a hundred of us, including myself," he said. "We are going to divide into three parties. McClintock will take twenty men and ride round the eastern slope of the hills, pick off the guards of the British horses and stampede the horses. Get among the horses, give them the whip and get them galloping. Capture a few if you want but scatter the rest. Drive them ten miles, at least before you give up.

"Donald Oge will take forty men and ride also around the eastern slope of the hills ten minutes behind McClintock. I, with forty others will go around the western slope of the hills. When McClintock raids the horses, the British will give the alarm and start out of the valley between the two hills. Donald Oge's men and mine will dismount and when the British come out, fire into them. Three rounds only, but let each man pick a target. After three rounds every man is to return to his horse and get away. If any of us are captured or wounded they will have to be left. If I am wounded or killed, Donald Oge will take command of the party. After him McClintock is to be in command. The rallying place will be Stickham's Fork to the east. If you have any questions, speak up now."

"If you are killed, it would be a hard thing for a Campbell to be under a Farqueson," said one of the men. "Since the Battle of Pinkie the Campbells have always had preference on the field over the Farquesons, as is well known."

Peter vaguely remembered from his history lessons the Battle of Pinkie. It had been fought some centuries before in Scotland.

"This isn't Scotland," he said, "and there are no Farquesons and Campbells and Frasers. There are soldiers of the Continental Army and that is all. Whoever I appoint to command—Farqueson, Campbell, Fraser, McGraw or Robertson, commands."

The men took the reply in silence but they plainly did not like it. They would follow Peter, perhaps for the very reason that he was not by blood one of them. But among themselves the historic preferences had to be observed. They weren't Americans yet. They were Scottish highlanders living in America.

"All right," said Peter. "McClintock, pick your men and go." The men McClintock picked came from his own valley. Donald Oge then made his selection. He took the rest of the men from his valley but had to fill up his number with Frasers and McGraws and this displeased both him and them.

Peter took the rest of the men and turned to Mr. Paddock.

"Cut your pony loose and ride with us," he said.

"And leave my whole library, representing a traveling university, here in the wilderness?" said Mr. Paddock, aghast.

"Yes," said Peter.

"But that would be an outrage," said Mr. Paddock.

"War is full of outrages," said Peter and added, "You

can come back after the raid and get your cart—if what you told me of Ferguson is true."

Mr. Paddock explained the situation to Aesop, then going to his cart made a selection of books to take with him should he be unable to return. Loaded down with books, which he stuffed into the pockets of his old-fashioned coat, he unharnessed the pony from the cart, climbed on her sleek back and followed behind Peter —as strange a figure in his huge top boots and oversize beaver hat as ever went to war.

For the next nine miles the three groups rode one behind the other. Then, Mr. Paddock having stated that they were approaching the British camp, McClintock sent off three men to scout and confirm the position of the British force. They were back in an hour, saying that all was as Mr. Paddock had stated.

"Can I go back to my cart now?" asked the bookseller.

"Yes," said Peter. "Go if you want."

"Ah, if I only had courage," said Mr. Paddock. "If I only had courage to stay and take part in the battle. But courage I haven't got and you would pity me sir, if you knew how much I suffer for the lack of it."

With that, he headed his pony back toward his cart, a lonely little figure with his beaver hat down over his ears and his pockets bulging with books.

## 7 ☆

The British encampment lay in a valley, as the book-seller had said, between two low ranges of hills. At the northern end of this valley was a flat meadow-like area, dotted with oak, pine and clumps of rhododendron. The southern end, where the horses were pick-eted, was narrow like the neck of a funnel, the distance between the two ranges of hills being no more than a hundred yards. This area with the hills so close on each side was a natural place for the horses to be kept, mak-ing it necessary to post guards only at the very end of the valley.

McClintock had been told to wait out of sight over the western range of hills until he was sure that Peter had got his men in place on the eastern range. The signal for attack was to be the firing of a single round from a rifle. Peter made his men dismount and leaving five in charge of the horses they crept to the brow of the hill. Lying down and peering over the top through the low shrubs which covered the hill, he could see the British guards below. There were six of them, not ten as Mr. Paddock had stated. One was sitting on a rock smoking a stub of clay pipe. He was not more than seventy yards away. The other five were standing at ease, their rifle butts on the ground and the barrels cradled in their arms. They were in a group close to the man who was smoking and were talking together.

Peter loaded his Deckhard and took aim at the seated man. But there was something about the way in which he was seated, so obviously enjoying his smoke that made it impossible for Peter to kill him. He raised the rifle slightly and squeezed the trigger. There was a flash from the pan, a jet of flame and smoke from the barrel and the seated man's hat was skipped off his head. Immediately McClintock's men, screeching like Iroquois braves on the warpath, came flying over the hill, a ragged bundle of mounted men, riding without benefit of reins and shooting as they rode.

Mounted they could get off only one volley, but the volley had a deadly effect. The clump of guards was suddenly crumpled to the ground, like so much straw stricken by a gust of wind. The horses they were guarding started to rear up and mill around, wheeling here and there. McClintock's men cut in between them and the British encampment, screeching and prodding the horses with their rifles to get them moving out of the valley.

For a moment it seemed to Peter that McClintock's party would be run down by the very horses they were trying to stampede. Then after whirling around and kicking and rearing, the horses started thundering out of the valley, the noise of their hoofs shaking the ground on which Peter lay.

McClintock and his men went after them still hallooing and screeching and soon the whole herd was out on the open ground and being chased away from the British camp. The first part of the plan had gone without a hitch. Of the British guards there was but one survivor —the man who had been smoking his pipe. When Peter had shot his hat off, he had flung himself on the ground, and so missed the volley that followed. He now took to his heels, running up the side of the hill, beyond whose ridge Donald Oge and his party were posted. He got almost to the top, there was a single report, and he crumpled to the ground rolled down a little way and then lay still. Peter felt a pang of regret. The death of this one lone man, running for his life, seemed at that moment utterly needless.

All this had occurred in a matter of two or three minutes. Now there came a rolling of drums from the British camp and a shrilling of flutes as the British in the valley were called to arms. They streamed out of their tents and with remarkable discipline formed immediately into companies.

Then they started out of the encampment through

the funnel end of the valley at the double, led by an officer in a green uniform whom Peter guessed to be Ferguson. When they got to the place where a few moments before the horses had been, they stopped, bewildered. The smoke of McClintock's volley was drifting up the hills born by a gentle wind. But no enemy were to be seen.

Ferguson shouted an order but Peter could not catch the words. It was apparently an order to skirmish about the area, for one company of men in extended formation went down the funnel of the valley, another company started to ascend the hill behind which Donald Oge and his men lay, and a third company started up the hill toward Peter.

"Drop them where they are," Peter ordered. The volley which followed was casual and calm. With each report, one of the enemy stumbled and fell, for they made an easy target for the mountaineers. Some stumbled back and collapsed and others fell forward. There was another volley from the hill opposite and the noise of the reports, coming from both sides, frightened the men who were caught in the narrow valley. They hesitated and then stopped and some started back down the hill. But hearing rifle fire behind as well as in front of them, their fear turned to panic and some of them ran back toward the encampment.

"Steady," shouted Ferguson, "steady." The words came clearly to Peter. The leisurely but killing fire continued and the panic spread. One man ran and then another. Soon they were running in twos and threes, back down the hills to the encampment from which they had come. The firing went on, but was not so telling now, for the gunpowder smoke made it hard to see a target.

Peter turned to the mountaineer nearest him. "Get to the horses," he said. "We've done our work." He went from man to man herding them ahead of him. Some of the men wanted to stay. They were excited and argued that more could be done if they fired a few more rounds. One man indeed, started back up to the brow of the hill and Peter had to drag him down by force. They got on their horses but not to retreat immediately, for Peter had one more thing he wished to do.

"Follow me," he cried and dug his heels into his horse, leading the men up the hill. They thundered all forty of them over the crest and down into the valley whose sides were now littered with bodies. On the valley floor Peter turned his horse so as to ride right through the British encampment. His men followed at full gallop, the hoofs of the horses flinging clods of earth behind them. There was a rattle of musketry but none of the rounds went home. Right through the encampment Peter and his men rode, scattering soldiers right and left. Peter stooped from his saddle, grabbed one British soldier under the shoulders and flung him across his horse in front of him. The man was too frightened to resist. When they had passed through the encampment and got a quarter of a mile beyond Peter reined in his mount and put the man down.

"Go on back," he said, "and tell them that Treegate's men made the raid. Remember the name. Treegate."

Then Peter dug his heels into his mount and went off at a gallop to Stickham's Fork, which was to be the rallying point.

When he got there he found McClintock was ahead of him. He had done what he was ordered and cut out twenty horses as spare mounts for the raiders. But Donald Oge had not returned. They waited for half an hour and then an hour before thirty of Donald Oge's men came in.

"Where are the rest," Peter demanded. "Where is Donald Oge himself?"

"Captured," said one of the men.

"How?" demanded Peter.

"It was the doing of one of the Frasers," said the man. "A Fraser should not be sent under the command of a Farqueson," he added accusingly.

"What happened?" demanded Peter.

"Donald Oge fired three rounds as you had ordered and then gave the order to retreat. And most of the men withdrew though some of them argued that it would be better to charge down and kill more of the Tories. But when Donald Oge told the Fraser to retreat, he said that the Farquesons could retreat if they wanted and it would not surprise him at all. But he being a Fraser would not retreat for the clan had the tradition in the old country that they were the first on the field of battle and the last off it. But that is not true for at Preston Pans it was the Frasers that broke first before Johnny Pope's men and the MacDonalds of the Isles that held the line, and the Farquesons helped them.

"That has always been a touchy point between the

Frasers and the Farquesons as any gentleman knows
and was the reason that this Fraser would not retreat
when Donald Oge told him.

"Indeed he called on the others to follow him down
the hill and give a charge at the Tories and never mind
Donald Oge who was a man so foolish as to put sense
before glory. And Donald Oge lost his temper and said
that by the living God there was no Fraser would get
deeper into the body of the enemy than himself, a Farqueson. And so the two of them went off with half a
dozen of their men with them and gave as pretty a
charge as I have ever seen and were captured. It was
myself, Ian MacInnes that rallied the rest of the men to
support Donald Oge and the Fraser and try to rescue
them. We drove the Tories back for a while but there
were too many of them. And so we came away and
came here. It is a pity you did not wait yourself, for if
you had attacked from the other side, Donald Oge
would not now be in danger of hanging."

"The devil with him and you too," cried Peter, very
angry. "If he had obeyed his orders he would not be a
prisoner and it is his own fault. By thunder if I ever get
my hands on him again I'll make him obey or send
him back where he came from in disgrace."

"You will be going back to rescue him then before
he is hung?" said the man hopefully. "He was no kin to
me but he is a bonny man and it is a pity to think of
such a fellow dangling on the end of a rope and the life
running out of him. Though," he added brightly, "he
might be shot and that would be more fitting for a gentleman of good family."

"I will not go back to get him," said Peter heatedly. "He is not more important than the other men I command here and I am not going to risk my whole force for him." He meant it when he said it, for he was filled with anger.

Ian MacInnes said nothing for a while, looking at Peter in a cold way. "If it were you that were captured," he said at length in a low voice, "Donald Oge would come and get you if it cost him his life. There is a difference between you and him and the difference is this—that he has a love for his men, but you have only a duty to your country." With that he turned on his heel and went off.

# 8 ☆

There was no immediate danger of pursuit by Ferguson again and make another raid. Peter's orders were to march on foot. Nor was there any likelihood that Ferguson would get new horses for his men. The countryside had been cleared clean of them, those not taken by the British being appropriated by the Continental militia and partisans. Yet there was the danger that Ferguson might be able, if a horse could be found, to send a man to Cornwallis to the south of him, and Cornwallis would detach a company of dragoons to seek and exterminate Peter's raiders. It was not an immediate danger, but one that would grow with the passage of time. The thing to do then was to make a big circle away from the area and moving to the north and then west contact Ferguson again and make another raid. Peter's orders were to entice Ferguson to King's Mountain. He must attack Ferguson and get away; attack again and get away again, until Ferguson, led deep into hostile territory would have to hole up on King's Mountain until relieved by Cornwallis.

That was the plan of Nollichucky Jack and reflecting on the plan, Peter began to see its merits. If Ferguson took to King's Mountain, then the Continental militia and irregulars could get there from Sycamore Flats before Cornwallis, and could attack Ferguson in overwhelming numbers and wipe out or capture his force.

Peter recalled something he had overheard just before the Battle of Trenton. The speaker was George Washington and he had said, "Weakness is a weapon, properly used. A weak force can control the movements of a stronger force by inviting pursuit. The leader of the weaker force is thus in command of the movements of a stronger enemy and this is one of the paradoxes of warfare."

It was true. Peter could control Ferguson. But he must keep his own little company intact. He must not risk an open battle. He must be always sure of getting away. And for this reason, an attempt to rescue Donald Oge was out of the question. This was one of the hard facts of war that the men did not understand. Not for the first time Peter realized the loneliness and isolation of a man in command.

He gave the order to move to the north and west and the men followed him in silence. McClintock, the big

McClintock he had beaten in the fight for the knife, rode beside him. The man had a dogged loyalty for Peter. He did not express it in words but in his attitude and actions. That he rode beside Peter now was an expression of this loyalty. He was the man who should have led the others to the rescue of Donald Oge for he was related to him by blood and came from the same valley. He did not, but instead rode beside Peter as a signal to the others they must support their leader whatever their personal feelings.

When they had been riding for an hour they came back into the same place where they had met Mr. Paddock, the bookseller, and a little further on, found him plodding ahead of them in his strange cart. At the sight of them, Mr. Paddock tried to get more speed out of his sleek pony, Aesop. But the animal was too well-fed and contented to have heart for anything so uncomfortable as a gallop. And Mr. Paddock had not the heart to lay a whip to his pony. All that Aesop would do was break into a gentle, matronly trot, and then settle down to a walk again. So Peter had soon caught up with him and reined in, halting his men.

"I trust sir," said Mr. Paddock, "that you return with the laurels of victory placed upon your brow, and indeed, I see your force intact and that you have several additional horses so I know this must be so."

Peter did not reply, but considered the little man, turning over a plan in his mind.

"Silence after victory," said Mr. Paddock. "You have indeed something of the classic hero in you sir, for you will recall that Phillip after Macedon said nothing for two hours, and Caesar stood in silence, staring at the plains of Egypt while his brilliant staff waited eagerly around, anxious for permission to congratulate him. Though there are some who say that Egypt was barely won and Caesar himself was aware of this and brooded on the matter." There was a certain shrewdness to this remark, as if Mr. Paddock had guessed that there had been a price paid for Peter's victory.

Peter still said nothing, reflecting on his plan. "You meditate while I chatter," said Mr. Paddock. "Forgive me. I have most of the time only Aesop to talk to and so have developed the knack of conversing with myself."

"Major Ferguson," said Peter. "He is a literary man?"

"Yes indeed," said Mr. Paddock. "A man whose noble mind is marred only by misguided loyalty to a faithless king."

"You can go to him without fear?" asked Peter.

Mr. Paddock hesitated.

"Never without fear sir," he said. "You mistake me. I am a coward and fear follows me like a shadow as others are livened by the golden halo of courage."

"Nonetheless, you can get to him unharmed."

"I believe I can," said Mr. Paddock.

"Good," said Peter. "Go to him and tell him to meet me with ten men as an escort and to bring my men with him."

"He will never do such a thing as that without good reason," said Mr. Paddock.

"He will have good reason," said Peter. "Tell him to reflect on the cry of King Richard at Bosworth Field as given in Shakespeare's play."

"A horse! A horse! my kingdom for a horse!" quoted Mr. Paddock.

"Yes," said Peter. "Tell him I will trade horses with him for my men he has captured."

Mr. Paddock removed his oversized beaver hat, wiped the nap of it with his elbow and replaced it on his head. This seemed to be a method of soothing his mind when he was agitated.

"Remarkable," he said. "I pronounce it quite remarkable. But you overlook the point sir, that Major Ferguson may blame me for your attack upon him, and hang me as a spy!"

"Come Mr. Paddock," said Peter, "you have assured me that Major Ferguson is a literary man and so he will hardly hang the proprietor of the only traveling university in the wilderness. Besides which, he at the present moment stands in uncommon need of horses."

"All right," said Mr. Paddock, "but I will say plainly that in this instance the horses and not literature will be the saving of me."

Off he went and Peter told his men to make camp where they were, and considered what he would say when and if Major Ferguson came to him. McClintock supervised the making of the camp and brought Peter a meal of that same parched corn, boiled to a pudding, off which he had breakfasted that morning. He sat beside him while Peter ate this and after a little while he said, "Donald Oge is a proud man."

Peter said nothing. He knew enough of the mountaineers to realize that the best way to get them to talk when something was on their minds was to be silent.

"Next to his father, Donald Mor, he is properly the leader of the people in his valley," said McClintock. He was squatting on his heels and looking at his big hands as if the sight of them gave him assurance and a mild pleasure.

"He should not have let the Fraser trick him into attacking the Tories," said McClintock, "and it would be proper if I had gone to his rescue. But I did not."

"Why?" asked Peter. He wanted to hear McClintock's reply in his own words.

"Because you are a better man than I am or Donald Oge and so I obey you," said McClintock. "It was not that you beat me in the knife fight, though that showed you were a better man than I. It was because you did not kill me but let me have the knife again and again. And then you did not scorn me but shook my hand. And that is why you are a better man than Donald Oge or I, for either of us would have killed you had the fight gone the other way. We knew you were a strange man and that is so."

"You should follow me because we both fight in the Continental cause," said Peter. "If you thought I was a worse man than you but I was appointed your leader by the Congress, you should follow me, because it is not the man that matters but the cause in which men fight."

"That may be so since you tell me it is," said McClintock. "And maybe some day I will agree with you because I will feel it myself. But I do not feel it now. You are the best man and after you comes Donald Oge and after that me. And since I am not better than

Donald Oge and am kin to him and owe him loyalty after you I want to make a bargain with you."

"What bargain?" asked Peter.

"Exchange me for Donald Oge," said McClintock, "and let me be hung instead of him." And he added with a certain simple shrewdness, "There would be a profit in it for they would free a good man and hang a worse one and there is a gain in that for us."

Peter was startled by the proposal which was made in all sincerity.

"I would never do such a thing," he said. "And let us have no more talk about good men and lesser men. In the Continental army there are only men who give orders and men who carry them out and that is all. What guards have you posted around the camp?"

"Ten men in pairs to the south of us," said McClintock. "And half a mile beyond that two men with two horses. It is from the south that we can expect an attack."

"Put men all around," said Peter. "Any man who posts guards only where he expects an attack is likely to be attacked in some other place."

McClintock went off to do as he was ordered and Peter turned again to reflecting on his plan to exchange horses for prisoners. He thought for a while of Nollichucky Jack and summoned MacInnes.

"Pick two men who know the country and have them ride to Sycamore Flats and tell Nollichucky Jack to start the militia moving towards King's Mountain," he said.

*9* ☆

Major Patrick Ferguson was a man unique in the British Army. Trained in the harsh discipline which Britain had imported from Hanover with her Hanoverian kings, he still had enough personality left to use his own imagination in pursuing, what was for him, the manly art of warfare.

Almost alone among British officers, he realized that warfare in the American wilderness was far different from warfare on the bloodied plains and fields of Europe. There, beautifully drilled armies lined up to face each other, withstood each other's cannon fire and hurled themselves at each other, line on line, with musket ball and then the bayonet.

But Ferguson realized from the start that no such

battles were likely to take place in the American war. Though the British redcoats and their German mercenaries might line up in magnificent battle formation, the Americans were likely to refuse to do the same, but cut them down with rifle fire, accurately directed from strategic positions selected by leaders used to Indian warfare. There would be little of the artillery barrage, and not much of the cavalry charge, no disciplined volleys followed by a flourish of bugles signaling the time to go in with the bayonet and finish the bloody work.

Realizing this, Ferguson had pleaded for and obtained permission to raise a corps of his own whom he called the American volunteers. They were indeed Americans—Americans who had sided with Parliament and King rather than Congress and Washington. Some had done this out of a deep and unshakable devotion to a sovereign whom they looked upon as their protector and to a land from which their fathers had come and for which they had fought against many enemies. Ferguson did not submit these Tories to the stern drill of the German drillmasters. Instead he trained them in the kind of fighting to which they were used. He picked expert riflemen, and used them as a flying column to raid Continental territory, fighting their fellow countrymen, also of the mountains and the frontier, who had thrown in their lot in the cause of liberty and the Continental Congress.

This then was the man that Peter Treegate met in the rain-drenched foothills of the Blue Ridge Mountains. Peter's message, baited with a reference to horses, had intrigued Major Patrick Ferguson, and he came with an escort of ten men and the prisoners taken during the raid on his encampment that morning. He was a small, trim man, hard as wire, with a lean face and a humorous look to his eyes. He wore the deerskin hunting shirt and leggings of the frontiersman, dyed green, and meeting Peter who towered over him by several inches said half in admiration and half jokingly, "You are not, I assume, General Washington in disguise?"

"No," said Peter. "Treegate is my name." And then because he wanted the name of Treegate to be spread about so that it would bring fear into the hearts of those who supported the King's cause he said, "It was I who raided your camp this morning."

"And very nicely contrived indeed," said Major Ferguson. "I confess myself horribly embarrassed. Still one learns by being wrong and you will not have that opportunity again." There was a little edge of menace in his tones and the bantering humor was gone.

"Not *that* opportunity," said Peter calmly, "but another opportunity and another and then another."

"Until I dispose of you," said Ferguson.

"If you can catch me," said Peter. Things were going well. Ferguson's pride had been hurt by the raid. Peter decided to aggravate the hurt for it would serve his purpose. "It is one thing to raid a few unarmed plantations, shoot or hang the men and then get away, Major," he said. "It is another thing to deal with a force of mountainmen better trained than your raggle-taggle Tories."

Beneath his sunburn Ferguson paled with anger.

"By thunder, sir," he said, "I find you insolent and I promise I will deal with you within the week."

"You must first catch me," said Peter calmly. "I recall that there was a British boast about having trapped General Washington at Trenton, but it was found that the fox had slipped the bag."

Ferguson was angry. So angry that he did not trust himself to reply for the moment. Good, thought Peter, he has pride, and pride, as Peace of God Manly has told me many a time, goes before a fall.

I will be able to lead him after me to where I want, and if I trade him a few horses now for Donald Oge and the other prisoners, he will have mounted scouts to keep an eye on where I am going and where I am camped. Only I won't be there when his unmounted men arrive to attack.

Donald Oge meanwhile had been standing with the other prisoners under guard of Ferguson's escort. He was feeling very sheepish and because he was sheepish adopted an attitude of impatience. Peter deliberately did not turn a look in his direction or say a word to him. He had a lesson to teach Donald Oge.

"Touching the reason for this parley," said Major Ferguson who had at last mastered his temper, "I got a message concerning horses and the bringing of these prisoners whom I was about to hang. I presume you are considering a trade."

"Yes," said Peter. "I need the men. I see there are six of them. What happened to the others?"

"Too wounded to travel, or dead," replied Ferguson.

"I have your word on that as an officer?" asked Peter.

Ferguson hesitated. "Some of them were shot against my orders," he said. "My men got momentarily out of hand. Three were I believe bayoneted. There is considerable hatred, as you are aware, between your men and mine—between loyal Americans and rebels against the king."

Peter nodded. There was no need to discuss the hatred. It stemmed from plunderings and burnings and hangings and shootings in ugly little raids by one side or the other, waged to settle private feuds as much as to advance the cause of one side or the other. He recalled the one lone Tory trying to get to safety up the hillside that morning and the single, callous rifle shot that had needlessly killed him. There were sins on both sides. War in the southern colonies was not always clean and brave. It could get vicious and cruel.

"You can give me the names of the men who are prisoners, who were shot or who are now gravely wounded?" he asked. Ferguson produced a piece of paper, torn from a journal with a list of names written on it.

"Here they are," he said. "And now about the trading of prisoners for horses. Three horses for every man would, I fancy, be suitable." He said the latter sentence carelessly as if he were stating a foregone conclusion. And because he said it in this manner Peter knew that he did not expect to receive such a ransom for the prisoners, and would bargain, though only after bluster.

"One horse for one man is what I had in mind," he said.

"That's ridiculous, sir," said Ferguson. "Surely you place a greater value on the lives of your comrades than one horse." He spoke loudly so that not only the prisoners, but Peter's men who were crowded around, could hear.

"One horse for one man," said Peter. "I will give you six horses and you will give me six men."

They had been squatting on their heels, facing each other. Ferguson rose slowly.

"You have wasted my time in bringing me here," he said. "I do not know why men should follow a leader who places so small a value on their lives." Again the voice was raised so the men could hear, and the words had their effect. The prisoners stared disgustedly at Peter and there was some muttering and uneasy shifting among the men, and hard looks.

"You have an urgent need of horses, Major," said Peter, still squatting on the ground. "You tramped six miles here to get them. I don't think you will be content to go away empty handed. And I am offering you six horses."

Ferguson did not reply. He motioned to the escort to take the men back. Then he said aloud and not to Peter, "It seems you have a leader who would willingly see his men hanged though he has it in his power to give them freedom so they can return to their families."

Peter was struck by the cunning of the man. Ferguson might indeed take the men back and hang them, feeling that he would secure a greater advantage by shaking the loyalty of Peter's men than by obtaining some horses. For a moment he was dismayed by the thought that Ferguson was winning a propaganda victory. If the men were hanged, Ferguson strangely enough would not now get the blame. It would be laid to Peter's charge and so it would richly reward Ferguson now to break off negotiations and take the prisoners back.

McClintock was squatting by Peter, saying nothing and avoiding the defiant and contemptuous stare of Donald Oge.

"Bring six horses," Peter said to him, and then louder than was necessary, "Perhaps Major Ferguson has forgotten, even in so short a time, what a splendid animal a good horse is."

Ferguson hesitated and did not give the command to march away with the prisoners. By hesitating he immediately lost the propaganda advantage that lay with him. Peter breathed more easily.

The horses McClintock brought were splendid beasts. There was one paint gelding with the fine small head of Arab breeding that immediately took Ferguson's eye. He gave a soft cluck and the horse came over to him. It was his own mount.

"Six horses for six men," said Peter.

"Twelve," said Ferguson.

"Six," said Peter firmly.

"I cannot let you have them for six," said Ferguson.

"All right," said Peter, "let us split the difference . . . nine."

"I must have twelve," said Ferguson but he was weakening and although he tried to make the statement sound final, it had no conviction.

"Let us go at this another way," said Peter. "Let us start trading man and animal." He pointed to one of the prisoners, ignoring Donald Oge. "I'll give you two horses for that man there." The man was the little bearded man who had been the spokesmen of the Farquesons the day Peter fought with McClintock. He was an excellent shot and an excellent scout.

Ferguson nodded. He had two horses for one man and liked the rate of exchange. Donald Oge glowered at Peter that he had not been the first one bargained for. Two other men were agreed on at two horses each. Donald Oge was white with anger. After some haggling a further man was exchanged for one horse. The next man was obtained for two leaving only Donald Oge still unransomed.

"What about him?" asked Ferguson.

"One horse," said Peter.

"But he led the second attack on my men," said Ferguson. He was watching Peter's face narrowly. There was something here he did not understand and he was curious.

"It is precisely for that reason that I am prepared to bid only one horse for him," said Peter. "He did it against my orders. He is not a man to be relied upon." There was a look of understanding in Ferguson's eyes and a trace of amusement. Seemingly he had faced and dealt with the same problem himself.

"Before God it was the damned Fraser that hinted I was a coward and so I lead the attack," stormed Donald Oge.

For the first time Peter looked at him.

"You are not a leader, Donald Oge," he said, "for other men can make you disobey orders. You betrayed the trust I had in you, betrayed your own honor and by your example encouraged the other men to betray me."

"It was not betrayal," stormed Donald Oge. "It was a matter of honor that you do not understand."

"Who are you to speak of honor," asked Peter calmly, "when you had not the honor to carry out the orders of a man who trusted you and put other men's lives in your hands? I am prepared to pay one horse for you. But that is out of humanity. You are not worth one horse. You are a danger to me and to the men who follow and fight with me. If Major Ferguson will trade you for a horse I will get your freedom and then send you back to the valley you came from. For you are no man of mine."

"But it was the damned Fraser who goaded me into the attack," cried Donald Oge.

"If you think you are a better man than the Fraser, you should have paid no heed to him other than report him to me," said Peter.

He turned to Major Ferguson.

"One horse," he said.

"One horse," said Ferguson and the bargain was made.

When Ferguson had gone with the horses Peter turned to McClintock.

"Tell the men to mount and follow me," he said. And then to Donald Oge he said, "Take whatever men are loyal to you and your ideas and go away with them. Let those that remain be loyal to me and the Continental cause. I want no others." He himself got on his horse and rode away, uncertain of how many would follow him, but conscious that he had done right.

## *10* ☆

Peter Treegate's raid had a disastrous effect on the plans of Major Patrick Ferguson. Without horses it was no longer possible for him to effect a speedy link with Cornwallis in the south. A journey which would have taken at the most three days would now take the better part of a week. He could still make the journey of course. But he was a man of pride, unbeaten in the field, and he did not want to appear before his commander-in-chief and confess that he had been defeated in a skirmish with a local force and had lost all his animals.

His pride demanded that he get his horses back, and so he must surprise Treegate and his raiders. He determined that he would do so and congratulated himself that he had obtained by an exchange of prisoners, ten horses. Scouts mounted on these would keep him informed of the whereabouts of Treegate and his men, and where they camped for the night. Then, with a forced march, he could and would surprise Treegate in his encampment, wipe out his force and recapture the horses.

This was precisely what Peter Treegate had planned. That night he camped in a small valley ten miles to the east—an easy march for the British. He ordered campfires lit and put pickets around the camp. But he dismounted the pickets and told them that they were not to shoot at intruders but to report their presence immediately. About nine that evening one of the pickets came in to report a horseman glimpsed for a moment on a ridge overlooking the camp. Another picket reported a further horseman on a ridge to the south. Peter let the men have three hours rest and then ordered them to mount but leave the fires of the encampment burning. They also left the shelters they had constructed standing as they withdrew and waited in the dark half a mile to the south of the camp.

An hour before dawn, Ferguson arrived. He had split his force, bringing four hundred with him and leaving the remainder to come on later. They went by, barely seen in the thin starshine which threw a faint glow on the men's musket barrels and bayonets, not more than a hundred yards from where Peter's men were hidden. They moved forward slowly toward the light of the fires and then there was a flourish on the bugle, a loud shrill cheer and they charged into the empty encampment.

They were hardly in it before Peter led his men at them. Mounted they thundered into the encampment, firing at whatever targets offered, bowling men over with their horses, and clubbing those who jumped for the reins.

The British were thrown into complete confusion, unable to form any line or establish any order with which to deal with the mounted raiders who hurtled at them out of the darkness. They were scattered like dust in a whirlwind, the thunder of the horses' hooves and the reports of rifles and muskets mingling with the shrieks of the wounded and the dying. All was over in a matter of three minutes. Peter led his men out of the little valley and away into the darkness to a rallying point half a mile away.

But the fact that Ferguson had split his command worried Peter. Somewhere further to the south was another and larger group of the Tories. Should he raid them also? Or should he withdraw leading Ferguson on closer and closer to King's Mountain.

The others of the party were for an attack. They were excited by their success—two victories over the great Ferguson in one day. They wanted more and were beginning to feel themselves invincible.

But Peter ruled against a further raid. The horses were weary and the men weary too though in their excitement they did not realize this. He ordered a further withdrawal to a camp in the fork of two rivers.

Here he rested his men for a day and a night and wondered what had happened to Donald Oge. After the exchange of prisoners Donald Oge had not come with Peter. He had left with ten men, and Peter assumed that he had decided to return to his valley.

On the morning of the second day news reached Peter that Nollichucky Jack and the other forces were moving toward King's Mountain. Peter had also sent scouts to keep an eye on Ferguson and they reported that he was moving south. He had, then, turned cautious, swallowed his pride and decided to link with Cornwallis instead of chasing Peter further. Peter was dismayed. All he could do was interpose his men between Ferguson and Cornwallis. But to do so would probably be without effect, indeed he might get caught in a pincer, trapped between Ferguson's Tories moving south and Cornwallis' men moving north to meet him. He doubted whether he could tempt Ferguson to chase him further. What was needed was a big display of force south on Ferguson between him and Cornwallis. It must be enough to convince the British commander that he could not hope to link up with his chief—that he must in short find a place of refuge until reinforcements could be sent to him.

Could Nollichucky Jack help? Peter sent him an urgent message describing the situation. He said that he would follow closely behind Ferguson and asked that Nollichucky make a major demonstration in front of the enemy to convince him that retreat was cut off.

An hour after sending off this message Peter led his raiders through the rolling hills in pursuit of Ferguson.

He came on him in a wide plain where there was no possibility of a surprise attack. Peter led his men parallel with Ferguson, in plain sight but out of accurate rifle shot. Toward noon Ferguson sent a party of about two hundred skirmishers toward Peter. It was a foolish move. Peter drew the skirmishers a mile and a half from the main body by retreating, then wheeled around and got between them and the main body of Ferguson's men. There was a brisk little battle in which Ferguson lost four killed and Peter one. The skirmishers withdrew, pursued by Treegate's raiders.

The game continued through the day but at dark Peter rode ahead of Ferguson and camped to the south of him, determined to cut off his passage if he could until Nollichucky Jack arrived. Nollichucky came with four hundred men toward dawn of that morning. He had ridden hard to get there and Peter told him the situation.

"He must come this way," said Nollichucky. "We'll wait for him here and give him such a hot reception he will think twice of going any further."

Ferguson was on the move an hour after dawn. He led his men in column over the brow of a low hill after having sent scouts ahead. The scouts had been allowed to pass unmolested. When the main body of Ferguson's men arrived it was allowed to approach to within fifty yards of Peter's position on either side of the trail. Then there was a sustained rattle of rifle fire, ripping through the brushwork and rocks behind which Peter's men were concealed. The Tories were flung into confusion for a few moments.

But they were well disciplined and soon deployed in extended order, so as not to be bunched together and offer a compact target. There was no panic among them. They fired deliberately, seeking a target for each round. A man next to Peter, who raised himself up for a moment, was hit squarely in the forehead and tumbled down dead with a look of mild surprise on his face. Another, shifting his position, incautiously exposed his arm and swore as a ball smashed through his elbow. Soon the still air was thick with musket smoke which drifted slowly over the scene of the battle. High above the smoke a little crowd of carrion crows circled awaiting a meal. The British started to creep forward, pressing a counterattack and Nollichucky, still wearing his bright blue coat, which in the circumstances made him a magnificent target, consulted with Peter.

"If they break through we can't hold them," he said. "But if we flank them, they will get away to the south which is the direction we don't want them to go in."

It was McClintock who offered a solution.

"It would be a good thing to take three hundred men and go half a mile south of here with them," he said. "There is a little valley that Ferguson will go through and if we are lined up across it and on either side we can stop him there and turn him as well. If a hundred men are left here to hold him for the time being, and then break before him, he will think he has the better of us and plunge on into the trap."

The plan was decided on and worked splendidly. Peter led the rear guard of a hundred riflemen, holding Ferguson while the others got in position. He retreated with his men slowly before Ferguson and then, pretending to panic, his men scattered. Ferguson took the bait and plunged straight on, so anxious to pursue that he got ahead of his baggage and ammunition carts. Peter rallied his men, cut off a few of the ammunition carts which were painted a bright red, stove in the casks of gunpowder and blew them up. Ferguson was well ahead when this happened, and already deep into the trap that Nollichucky had set for him. When he heard the gunpowder blow up in his rear, he turned but it was too late. There was a storm of fire from both sides and in front of him and he and his men went reeling back in the direction from which they had come. Ferguson had now only one place to which he could make to defend himself—King's Mountain. He made for it as fast as he could, unaware that this was the spot selected for a showdown by his enemies.

*II* ☆

King's Mountain lies on the border of North and South
Carolina, a place deserving the name of a mountain
only in that it forms a bold feature of a rolling and
desolate landscape, full of pine scrub and boulders and
streams which extend about for many miles. Above this
inhospitable area, like a fort constructed by nature, the
mountain stands. But in no other part of the world would
it be dignified by such a name. Its eroded sides, heavily
timbered with pines and studded with boulders of red
sandstone and granite, are scarcely a hundred feet high.
The top is in the shape of a lengthy oblong, five hundred yards on its greatest axis and seventy to eighty
yards wide, though broadening to a hundred-and-
twenty yards at one end. This top is flat and around its

edges studded with trees. In retreating to it Major
Ferguson believed that he could hold the position in-
definitely until relieved. Once on the mountain top he
boasted that he would defy God Almighty and all the
rebels out of hell to overcome him. The boast, though
blasphemous, might be militarily justified. Whoever
tried to storm his position must scale the steep sides of
the mountain into the face of a murderous fire from
Ferguson's riflemen. Further, although Peter's raiders
had destroyed some of his stores, he still had a plentitude of gunpowder and shot. His men were equipped
with bayonets and charging down the short slope of the
mountain could drive back with cold steel any who
tried to gain the top. He had overlooked only two fac-
tors—the hatred of himself and his men by the Americans, many of whom had seen their relatives hanged
by Ferguson's Tories, and the fact that the pine growth
around the flanks of the mountain offered more protection to the attackers than the defenders.

Ferguson reached King's Mountain in full retreat on
October 6, 1780. Close on his heels came Nollichucky
Jack and Peter Treegate, with four hundred men at
their backs. By noon of October 7th the rest of the
patriot army had come up, a hundred and sixty men
under fiery Charles McDowell of North Carolina, two
hundred and forty "over mountain" men, bearded,
rough and taciturn under Colonel Isaac Shelby and
four hundred Virginia frontiersmen under big John
Campbell.

There was no need for a council of war as the Americans numbered over twelve hundred. They were for

the most part mounted. They tethered their horses, tied their blankets to the saddles and filed off under their various leaders to occupy a position at the foot of the mountain, so that when they were all in place at the foot, Ferguson at the top was ringed about by twelve hundred men bent on his extermination. The fox had been treed, as Nollichucky Jack had planned. It remained to be seen whether he could still get away.

Before the attack a strange silence settled over both armies. There was no wind and so no rustling of the pines, whose branches were motionless as if in some terrible expectancy. It was so quiet that Peter could hear from around the mountain the slight clanging sound of the men ramming charges into their rifles in preparation for the fight. Then he heard, quite distinctly, a series of little clicks as hammers were cocked. And then silence interrupted by only a cough here and there and an occasional whisper which seemed to carry like a shout through the brooding air.

Then from the other side of the mountain came the wild rising screech of the Iroquois war whoop. It was taken up in a moment by the men at the foot of the mountain—a horrible high-pitched wavering cry that culminated in a series of whoops and made the skin of Peter's scalp crawl though he had heard the war shout many times. From the top of the mountain came a thunder of drums as Ferguson called his men to arms.

"Shout like hell and fight like devils," big John Campbell who was on Peter's left cried and the two of them started up the side of the mountain, rifles held high for balance and scrambling for a footing. For perhaps a

minute nothing happened. Peter got within ten feet of
the top and suddenly over the brim poured a horde of
Tories, firing as they came. He shot from the hip and
toppled one. The bullets hummed around him like bees,
clipping pine twigs which fell to the ground like a
shower of sudden rain. The Tories came on with the
bayonet, and Peter clubbed his rifle to deal with them.
He drove the butt into the chest of one man, ducked a
shining bayonet, dropped his rifle and drew his hunting
knife. He was an expert with the knife, well taught by
his foster father the Maclaren of Spey. What followed
was an ugly hand-to-hand engagement, bayonets versus
hunting knives and rifle butts. Finally Peter and his
men were driven back to the foot of the mountain and
the initial assault had failed. It was immediately followed however by another assault on the other side of
the mountain where Campbell led his Virginians in an
attempt to gain the top. Four hundred of them swarmed
up the sides, and gained the rim of the mountain only
to be driven back by the bayonets of Ferguson's Tories.
But Campbell's men took shelter behind the pines and
boulders that littered the slope and, reloading their rifles,
fired to such an effect that the Tories had to retreat.
Immediately another assault was launched by Colonel
Isaac Shelby and Peter, having rallied his men, led
them again in an attack. Now Ferguson had to defend
himself against several assaults launched simultaneously.
The rim and sides of the mountain all around burst into
a vicious wall of jets of flame and puffs of smoke. The
smoke remained in an increasing cloud, there being
no wind to carry it away and Peter, enveloped in it,

lost touch with his men and could not see the enemy ahead of him. From his left and slightly above him, he heard a loud cheer, signaling that one party of attackers had gained the mountain top. He struggled up himself, his rifle clubbed; felled a man who loomed out of the smoke before him, pressed on, was flung to the ground by a huge boulder that came rolling down from the top, regained his feet and suddenly found himself on the top of the mountain where the cloud of gunpowder smoke thinned, for being heavy it tended to roll down the sides. All on the top of the mountain was in a state of wild confusion. Groups of men were struggling in small, horrible battles swinging at each other with rifles. No quarter was being asked or given. The Tories retreated from the mountain rim toward the center and one of them managed to raise a white flag. It was immediately snatched down by Major Ferguson who shouted "No surrender to rebels." In the first moments after the mountain top was gained the fighting was hand-to-hand. Men grappled with each other and tumbled down the mountain side locked together. But as the Tories retreated to the center, forming a hopeless and bewildered mob of men, the attackers loaded their rifles and forming a ring about them, fired into them. Again a flag of surrender was raised and again Peter saw Ferguson fight his way toward it and pull it down. One man tried to haul down the English colors and Ferguson pistoled him to the ground. Then he placed his back to the flagpole and shouted his defiance, trying to encourage his men to sweep the invaders off the mountain top. One party of the Tories rallied sufficiently to make a dash with the bayonet at the ring of the attackers around them. They charged out of the mass of their fellows cheering, with Ian Farqueson, the brother of Donald Oge at their head. Peter recognized immediately the man who had sworn to take his life. Farqueson saw him and with a bellow charged toward Peter. His face was livid with fury and he had a long hunting knife, called among the Scot mountaineers a *sgean mor*, or big knife, in his hand. When he was only a few feet away he whipped back his arm and flung the knife. The action was so unexpected that Peter had no time to duck and the blade embedded itself in his shoulder causing him to drop his own knife. Then Ian Farqueson was on him, throwing him to the ground and pulling out his tomahawk. Peter saw the wicked blade of the tomahawk poised over him against the brooding sky and tried desperately to get away. But the man had his knee on Peter's upper arm and pinned him to the ground. Just when he expected the blow to fall, Ian Farqueson toppled back off him, his face gushing blood. Peter rolled the dead man away and got to his feet. A few yards away he saw Donald Oge, the dead man's brother, reloading his rifle and knew who had saved his life.

"Your own brother!" cried Peter.

"My enemy and yours," said Donald Oge. He knelt by the side of his brother and turned him over to look at his bloodied face. Then he made a cross on his brother's forehead with his thumb and when he turned to Peter again his face was hard set but tears were streaming down his cheeks.

"A curse on the day that brought this death," he said and buried his head on his brother's chest, the sobs shaking his whole frame. The exultation of the victory drained out of Peter. He felt sick and utterly lonely and walked away from the dead man and his brother, careless of the fighting around or the wound to his shoulder.

The victory was indeed won but now came the slaughter. Up to this point what had happened had been a battle fought in the course of a revolution against an oppressive power. What followed was revenge—a merciless and bloody extermination of men individually hated by their enemies. In the southern colonies the war was besides a revolution a civil war in which brother fought brother and father fought son and planters and farmers rejoiced at the pillage and burning of their neighbors' property. Blood ran hot and hate ran high and part of the harvest was to be reaped now on the summit of King's Mountain.

The Tories, after the failure of the counterattack led by Ian Farqueson had been thrust back into the center of the plateau and were ringed around by the Continentals. These men, some from over the mountains and some from the foothills and plains, some from Camden and Winnesboro and Charleston—merchant and mountaineer, farmer and man of business, but all with personal scores to settle, now poured a frightful fire from their rifles and muskets into the mob of their enemies. Shouts of surrender and pleas for quarter were met with shouts of scorn and jibes without pity.

"Quarter! Quarter!" cried the Tories.

"Tarleton's Quarter! Ferguson's Quarter!" mocked the

victors. They referred to the shooting, bayoneting and hanging of their fellows by the men of both Tarleton and Ferguson. And they continued to fire away until the outer rim of the mob of encircled prisoners was heaped high with bodies, some dead and some dying, behind which the others sought to protect themselves.

"In God's name don't kill me," one man cried holding up his arms.

"I know you Reuben Ames," was the reply. "You laughed while my father was hanged," and the man went down shot through the chest.

Peter, sickened by the death of Ian Farqueson, heard all the tumult and the firing and saw what was happening. Nollichucky Jack, Campbell and Shelby were trying in vain to get their men to stop the shooting of the Tories who had surrendered, but in vain. His arm drenched with blood from the knife wound, Peter knocked up the rifles of the men who were firing into the mass of the Tories. It was useless. The blood lust was on them. They swore at him and went on firing. One even turned his rifle on Peter and would have shot him, his face contorted with fury, but for McClintock. The big mountain man had become separated from Peter in the storming of the mountain, but found him now. He downed the man who threatened Peter with a blow to the chest that was enough to have felled a horse. Then he shouted above the tumult, "Treegate's men! Treegate's men! Over here." They came in ones and twos. Some of them were the very men who had been firing into the prisoners. Peter looked at them, bewildered but proud that they had answered the call to his name. Donald Oge was among them, standing in the fore. But Donald Oge was looking to Peter now for orders with a kind of anxiety in his eyes, as if pleading to be given some commission, the more dangerous the better.

"Protect the prisoners," Peter said and led the men, with their rifles to the pile of growing bodies. One or two of them were hit as they walked into the circle of fire. They turned and faced their own comrades and Peter shouted. "Cease firing or we will fire on you."

The order was met with jeers and shouts of "Renegade" and "Traitor."

"One volley, high," Peter shouted and his men brought up their rifles. Immediately the others stopped their firing, perhaps in amazement, perhaps because they were beginning to sicken at the sight of their own handiwork.

"Fire," shouted Peter and the rifles rattled as the rounds swept over the heads of the others. They fell back but one of them, stooping low, brought his rifle up to shoot Peter. Donald Oge saw him and with a shout flung his tomahawk and the man went to the ground with the thrown ax in his shoulder.

That was the end of the slaughter. It had needed an interval of only a moment to be stopped by its own horror. The Continentals still glared their hatred of Ferguson's men. But they contented themselves with jeers and threats. There was only one more death. Major Ferguson had continued fighting around the still unlowered British flag. Finally an aide managed to convince him that further resistance was useless. Still he would not surrender. There was a horse nearby, bleeding from a few wounds but still not lamed. Ferguson flung himself on it, dug his spurs into the animal's sides and tried to break through the wall of enemies who surrounded him. But he was hardly in the saddle before there was a fusillade of shots and he fell to the ground with a dozen bullets in him. The fright-crazed horse galloped off, dragging the dead rider along the ground for Ferguson's foot had caught in a stirrup when he fell. Then the horse was brought down and steed and rider lay dead together on the top of the mountain that Ferguson had boasted he would defend against "God Almighty himself and all the rebels out of hell."

Only one mercy was granted Ferguson. When he died the British colors were still flying. They were hauled down only after the life had gone out of him, and a Continental flag replaced them against the boding sky.

That night the rain fell in torrents and rolled in a flood down the sides of King's Mountain. It was a red tide, some said from the sandstone of the mountain's sides, others from the blood of those who had died on its terrible flattened top.

*12* ☆

Of the Tories who had fought at King's Mountain none escaped. Those not killed were captured so that this vicious battle resulted in the complete extermination of Ferguson's force. It was one of the ironies of the war that the only Englishman engaged in the Battle of King's Mountain was Major Ferguson himself. The rest of the men on both sides were American-born.

Lord Cornwallis received the news of the disaster at Charlotte, North Carolina. He received it from the man whom he had sent to Ferguson's relief, a man even more hated by the Continentals than Ferguson—Lieutenant Colonel Banastre Tarleton. Tarleton, approaching King's Mountain, heard of the extermination of

Ferguson's men and turned about and galloped pell-mell back to Cornwallis with the news.

"The whole countryside is up in arms against us, and every confounded farmer or planter with as much as a squirrel gun to his name has plucked up the courage to fire at us on our way here," Tarleton fumed.

Cornwallis said nothing. His normally pleasant face was grave, for perhaps alone in the whole British command he realized the gravity of the news. It was not just a case of a battle lost. It was, he sensed, the turning of a tide and that tide which had now set against him might reach a flood and overwhelm him soon if he did not act with vigor immediately.

"I do not understand why Ferguson made for King's Mountain instead of linking up with me," Cornwallis said. "There must have been something to prevent him."

"There was," said Tarleton. "A rebel by the name of Treegate. If half the stories that are around the countryside about him now are true, he is a combination of Hercules and Samson with something of Solomon and his wisdom thrown in. This Treegate, with a band of mountain men, raided Major Ferguson's camp, captured all his horses, then had the audacity to trade a few horses for prisoners, and finally so harried Ferguson that he was obliged to take refuge on King's Mountain where he met his end."

"Treegate," said Cornwallis. "Treegate. I have heard of Marion and Shelby but the name Treegate is new to me."

"He's everybody's hero now," said Tarleton. "He's supposed to be a giant of a man and one of the few

rebel leaders who is able to handle the Scottish mountaineers. Apparently he was brought up among them
as a boy though his people come from Boston. He is
supposed to be proof against lead or steel but not
against the hangman's rope."

"And where did you get that interesting piece of information?" asked Cornwallis in his quiet English voice.

"A couple of his men captured by Ferguson," said
Tarleton. "They come from over the mountains and
heard a woman there warn Treegate against the rope.
There is sometimes something to what these old crones
say. The half of them are hags in league with the devil
in my view."

"Come, Tarleton," said Cornwallis, "a man of your
education will hardly put any faith in witchcraft and
old wive's tales."

"In my club in London I do not believe these things,"
said Tarleton. "Out here in the wilds—well, it is another matter. In any case, the thing to do with Treegate
is to capture him and hang him."

"There have been too many hangings already," said
Cornwallis. "If there were fewer, we would have fewer
enemies."

"I beg to disagree," said Tarleton. "If we had hung
more, we would have struck more fear into these
damned rebels and they would not be so quick to rise
against us. In any case, if Treegate is to be dealt with, it
should be soon, before he is such a popular hero that
people will rally to his very name. A quick capture and
a quick hanging would save us a lot of trouble."

Cornwallis nodded. "Bear it in mind," he said.

"Meanwhile King's Mountain cannot go unavenged. We must meet the main body of the enemy and smash them. There is no other choice. To remain inactive now would be to encourage rebellion just at the moment when it must be exterminated completely."

Peter Treegate, Nollichucky Jack and the other leaders of the partisans had meanwhile retreated to Hillsboro in North Carolina, there to link up with the main body of the Continental Army still commanded by the unfortunate General Gates.

Peter's arm was in need of a surgeon's care. The day after the battle it was heavily inflamed. Ian Farqueson's knife had penetrated the muscles at the pit of the arm and Peter had bled heavily from the wound. By the time he arrived at Hillsboro he was scarcely able to remain in the saddle. There a surgeon examined the wound and said that it must be drained of pus and then cauterized. The operation, he pronounced, must be done immediately, lest, as he put it, the "canker enter the joints of the bone setting up a noxious humor which would invade the whole system."

The surgeon was a small, very thin man, with a face heavily marked by smallpox. His long nose was so pitted that it seemed as if someone must have taken an awl and gouged out pieces of the flesh all along its length. He was furthermore blind in one eye and somewhat deaf—both these handicaps being the result of the same smallpox which had nearly cost him his life.

He called for hot water and compresses and laid

Peter, stripped to the waist, on a table of planks which was by no means clean. McClintock was with Peter but he would plainly rather have been somewhere else, for his face was ashen. The surgeon opened a wooden case containing his instruments and selected a lancet which he stropped a couple of times on the sole of his shoe and then gave a quick rinse in a basin of water. Then he put the lancet on the table, fished a small snuffbox out of a pocket in the tail of his coat, and took a pinch of snuff between fingers yellowed from its use.

"Would you like a pinch yourself, sir?" he asked, offering Peter the snuffbox. "It is a Turkish variety and excellent for clearing the brain."

Peter groaned and shook his head, and the surgeon, having inhaled his snuff and sneezed copiously twice, picked up the lancet with a flourish, thrust it into the scar tissue which was forming over the wound, and opened the whole with a quick flick of the blade.

Immediately a quantity of blood and pus came out and the surgeon applied pressure to the surrounding areas so that the perspiration streamed off Peter's face from the pain. The wound having been drained, the surgeon next heated his irons to cauterize it, telling McClintock to hold Peter while this was done. He then inserted drains of cotton, twisted into a piece of string, in the wound, applied hot compresses and told Peter to return the following afternoon when he would examine it again.

"You are lucky it was not a bullet that caused the wound," he said. "The flesh may readily withstand steel, but lead contains many poisons and a bullet left in your arm for twenty-four hours would cost you the use of the limb."

The next day Peter's arm was no longer inflamed. The surgeon was delighted and it seemed to Peter somewhat surprised. He wanted to open the wound once more with his lancet and cauterize it further, for he said plainly the cauterizing with the hot irons had effected the greater part of the healing. But Peter would have no more of this treatment and refused to co-operate. The surgeon grumbled and then asked Peter to sign a statement testifying that the operation was successful.

"I have my degree from the University of Milan," he said. "But took it in horse doctoring and to tell you the truth was unable to build up any medical practice before I joined the Continental Army. You would do me a distinct service if you would sign an affidavit saying I cured your wound, for the war will not last forever and a man must look to what lies ahead of him when peace comes."

"You mean to tell me that you are a horse leech but you signed on with the Continental Army as a doctor?" demanded Peter.

"I am not alone in this, I assure you, sir," replied the surgeon. "Indeed I can point to an unimpeachable precedent, for George Washington himself was but a planter and yet he signed on as a General. And has done creditably in the role, as we all know."

Peter signed the affidavit which the doctor put away with a number of others he had obtained against the time when he would start a private medical practice at the end of the war.

"You may take the drains out of the wound in a day or two," he said. "But if there is any return of inflammation, I pray you come back to me and I will cauterize again."

Peter removed the drains the next day and the wound was well on the way to being healed in a week, though he was required to keep his arm in a sling to prevent it from opening until it had knitted.

For the next few weeks there was not much activity in the Carolinas on either side. Tarleton, anxious to revenge King's Mountain, pushed with a few hundred raiders to Blackstone's plantation near the Tiger River, and got a severe drubbing at the hands of Nollichucky Jack. Peter was not sufficiently recovered to be with Nollichucky at this engagement. Then there came news that Cornwallis was preparing to thrust northward against the Continentals and had been reinforced for this purpose. And shortly after that a new commander arrived for the Continental Army—the kind of man Peter had ridden north to seek after the disaster of Camden.

His name was Nathaniel Greene—a man of medium build with dark, curly hair and a solemn look to him. He rode into the camp at Hillsboro with a staff of officers from the northern army and the mountain men looked him over as he went by and wondered whether he would prove to be another Gates. He spent only a night at Hillsboro, and then went on to Charlotte,

North Carolina, taking the men from Hillsboro with him.

It was at Charlotte that the unfortunate Gates had his headquarters and here Gates turned over his command officially to Greene. The command on paper consisted of two-thousand-three-hundred infantrymen, sixty gunners and ninety cavalrymen. The mountaineers with horses were not included on Gates's rolls at all for he had seen fit to ignore them completely. But Greene quickly made it clear that matters would now go differently. Gates had hardly taken his departure before the new commander summoned a meeting of officers—partisan leaders as well as regular officers of the army and the militia.

"Gentlemen," he said. "I am here to fight and that is what I propose to do, with your help. We have all of us one cause, whether we serve with the Continental line, the State Militia or the irregulars. That being so, let us work together, consulting with each other on all matters and co-operating with each other to the fullest extent.

"I have been looking over the rolls and comparing them with the men who are fighting fit. The rolls speak of some two thousand men. Of these I find that there are only about eight hundred who are properly clothed and armed and fit to fight. And these men are largely demoralized and have forgotten their discipline. Order must be restored, clothing and arms found for them. This will take time and in the meantime the enemy must be held."

He looked now to the partisan leaders who were

seated to the left of the tent where the conference was taking place.

"Until the regulars are fit to fight," he said, "I must ask you gentlemen to take the initiative against the enemy. But you will not be without whatever support I can give you. We have against us some four thousand of the enemy, fully equipped and well trained. Including forces of irregulars we ourselves, at the present moment, can muster perhaps two thousand effectives. In this situation, I have decided to split my army in two."

The effect of this statement, calmly delivered, was electric. The officers stared at each other, wondering whether they had heard aright. Peter glanced at Nollichucky Jack and saw that Nollichucky was grinning, though at what, Peter could not then understand.

One of the regular officers broke the stunned silence that followed, by saying, "Split your army, sir—in the face of a superior force? That is contrary to all the rules of strategy."

Greene nodded. "I am aware of that," he said. "And the decision is a desperate one, but one to which I find no alternative. Cornwallis is securely in possession of South Carolina and Georgia. He proposes to drive into North Carolina and secure that state. Then the road to Virginia and Pennsylvania is open to him. We are not strong enough to block his path. We dare not give him battle. But if I split my force and move a portion of it on his flank to the west of him, then he must follow suit. He must split his army too. And what he will have left will not be sufficient to carry out his plan of driving deep into North Carolina."

Nollichucky slapped his hand on his thigh, highly delighted. The noise was plainly heard and several looked over at him. General Greene among them.

"I see there is at least one among us who approves of my plan," he said. "May I look for support from others?"

He got his support from the partisan leaders. They were men who did not fight by a book of rules, but devised their own rules to suit the circumstances. The regular officers were dismayed. Their textbooks plainly told them that to divide an inferior force in the face of an enemy was to invite disaster. They were, in short, fearful of their new leader.

"I do not pretend to omnipotence," said General Greene solemnly, "and it is possible that what I propose to do may result in complete disaster. Has anyone then any alternative plan to offer?"

This was a chance for the regulars to make their own proposals and some of them did. They were listened to closely. One suggested waiting several weeks, if need be, until reinforcements arrived from the north.

"I expect reinforcements," said General Greene, "but I have been warned that there will not be many. It is the opinion of General Washington that the issue of the war will be decided in the northern department. He is not to be blamed if he is unwilling to weaken the army above New York to strengthen us here."

Another suggested an attack on Cornwallis immediately.

"We cannot afford to risk the whole of the southern colonies on a single victory or defeat," replied General

Greene. "We are not strong enough to ensure victory and defeat would mean the end of the struggle in the south."

There were no other suggestions of importance to be made. The decision then was to detach a large portion of General Greene's force, under the command of General Daniel Morgan, and send it to the west, ostensibly to attack the British fort at Ninety Six.

"If I know Cornwallis well enough," said General Greene, "he will divide his force too, and send perhaps as many as a thousand men to protect Ninety Six. If he does that, we will already have gained a strategic victory, for he will not have enough men left to proceed with the invasion of North Carolina."

"What do you think of our new commander?" Peter asked Nollichucky Jack when they left the conference.

"I think that at last we have been sent a man we can win with," replied Nollichucky. "And I'll tell you something more. I think General Washington is wrong, and that the war will be won, not in New York, but here in the southern colonies."

"Maybe you're right," said Peter. "But ever since the war started, we have never had enough men, and they have always been in the wrong place."

"What brings victory," said Nollichucky, "is having the right number of men in the right place at the right time for the last battle. All other defeats and mistakes don't matter."

*13* ☆

The winter rains now commenced in earnest, turning the rivers into floods and the land between them into bogs of sticky mud in which horses sank over their fetlocks and men marched with the mud up to their calves.

Daniel Morgan was an old hand at campaigning in this kind of weather. He was a tall, grizzled man, a pioneer of Indian fighting and Braddock's disastrous campaign against the French in the French and Indian Wars. He had served with the Redcoats then as a loyal subject of the British king. But his independence of spirit had got him into trouble and he had been lashed to a gunwheel as a young man and flogged for some minor breach of discipline. The scars left by the horse-whip which had been used on him still showed as livid streaks on his torso.

At the outbreak of the Revolutionary War, he had thrown in his lot with the Continental Army, fighting in every major battle up to Saratoga. Then, passed over time and again when promotions were approved by the Congress, he had quit the Continental service in disgust. But when he got news of Gates's defeat at Camden, he put his personal hurts aside and rode several hundred miles to place his services at the disposal of Gates, who largely ignored him, for General Gates, among his many failings, had no idea how to employ irregular troops.

Greene was a different kind of man altogether and in selecting Morgan as the leader of that section of his divided army assigned the task of menacing Cornwallis on his left flank, he picked precisely the right man for the job and assured the irregulars that from now on their importance would not be ignored.

Morgan picked his own men for the task. He took Nollichucky Jack and Peter Treegate and the men who followed these two, plus his own frontiersmen and filled his force up to the number of a thousand with militia. He took Nollichucky and Peter aside privately before starting on his march.

"It is the militia who are the weakest among us, look you," he said in his Welsh accent. "There is not one of them that is not gunshy and the sight of the enemy charging on them takes away all their manliness and they run. How are your own men? Have they any fear on them when the enemy sound the charge?"

"I have the opposite trouble with mine," said Peter. "I cannot get them to retreat when a retreat is what is called for."

"They are from the mountains, isn't it?" asked Morgan.

"Yes," said Peter. "And they carry their clan feuds with them, though I think I have taught them a lesson." He related the story of how he had humbled Donald Oge.

"That was well done," said Morgan, "but watch you do not hurt the man too much, or he will turn on you to save his pride."

"I have given him back his command," said Peter. "But I have told him that if he disobeys orders once again, I will send him back to his own valley in disgrace."

Morgan nodded and turned to Nollichucky. "How about your men?" he asked.

"They have known me for years and will follow me anywhere," was the reply.

"Good. Then both of you keep an eye on the militia. Let your men know quietly that we must expect the militia to run, but they themselves are to stand firm. If we can get the militia to fire two rounds, that is all we can expect of them. They will take to their heels and that will be the end of them."

"If they are going to run away," said Peter, "why not give them orders to run? Why not tell them to stand firm for two rounds and then withdraw? If everyone knew they were ordered to withdraw then it would not demoralize the rest when they saw the militia leaving."

"You have a good head on your shoulders there," said Morgan. "I will bear what you say in mind. But both of you do what you can to help the militia so that there is some spirit of comradeship built up between them and your own men."

The militia were certainly in need of help on the terrible march ahead. Merchants, farmers, shopkeepers— there was not one of them accustomed either to warfare or to being abroad in such vile weather. The rain started with the march, and did not lessen for three days and nights. The militia, clad in woolen clothing and without topcoats, were drenched to the skin and remained drenched. Some of them were without boots and marched barefoot. Their feet were tender and they hobbled pitifully along, using their muskets as crutches to help them. They stumbled repeatedly and often fell full-length in the mud which covered them from head to foot. They were bruised in every bone. Some quit, sneaking off to their homes in the night. No attempt was made to bring them back. The frontiersmen were contemptuous of creatures so little able to fend for themselves in a storm.

Peter mustered his men to help the militia but they would not do so until he himself took two muskets and carried them himself. Then McClintock took a militiaman's musket and then Donald Oge, though not with any great grace. Soon Peter's men were carrying not only their own arms but those of many of the militiamen as well. When it came to fording rivers, militiamen were as helpless as sheep.

The rivers were very swollen by the rains, and fast flowing. Trees and limbs of trees were swept down by the current, knocking men down in midstream or carrying them away. The mountain men knew enough, when struck by a waterlogged tree in this manner, to go with it rather than fight it, and then land further down. The militiamen screamed, fought, went under and drowned in panic.

At the Catawba, which was the broadest stream that had to be crossed, twenty of the militia were drowned before a rope could be gotten across to which they could hold. A few river boats were rounded up to get the horses over, but men clung to the sides of these and swamped one. The horses threshed and whinneyed in the muddy swirling water and would have been carried away but for the mountain men. They got on their backs, knowing that despite the weight, a horse felt safe with a rider on him. Only one horse was lost in the Catawba crossing but two small cannon mounted on tripods and called, because of this, "grasshoppers" went to the bottom.

Peter thought they ought to destroy the barges when they got to the other side, but Morgan ruled differently. "Leave them," he said.

"But Tarleton and his men will use them to cross after us," said Peter.

"That is what I am hoping," said Morgan with a wink. "It would not suit me at all to have us on one side of the river and Tarleton on the other. We must draw him as far away as we can from Cornwallis and then when he cannot be reinforced, we will turn on him."

"You would not, I suppose, have picked a place where we will turn on him?" asked Nollichucky.

"I have," said Morgan. "You know the Cowpens?"

Nollichucky nodded. The Cowpens were not far from King's Mountain. The name was given to an area where cattle were commonly penned overnight while being driven to market.

"We will wait for him there," said Morgan. "There is a nice piece of river that will protect one flank and our rear and there is good open ground in front for the enemy to advance over, and two good little hills for us to take up our position on.

"And the thing I like best about Cowpens is that there is no swamp or brush nearby. And the reason I like that is that there is thus no place for the militia to run into and hide. I will give them orders to run, as you suggested, Captain Treegate. But if there was a swamp handy, they would run before they got their orders and that would be no use whatever."

"You have no great opinion of the militia," said Peter.

"I have as good opinion of them as I have of any un-trained soldiers," said Morgan. "No group of men have more courage than another. The difference is in dis-cipline and discipline is what the militia haven't got. But there can be too much discipline too, that deprives a man of the use of his own brains. The Redcoats have too much discipline and so will do anything they are told, except think for themselves. And therein lies their weakness and our strength."

So the terrible march went on in the unceasing rains.

Drenched during the day, the men slept still drenched at night. For food they had only soaked bread, partly cooked meat and a mush of corn. They drank water in which there was always mud, and many of the men developed dysentery and dragged themselves along more dead than living. Shortly after crossing the Catawba, Morgan ordered a few carts left behind. Horses that went lame were abandoned too, to the disgust of the mountain men.

"It is foolishness to leave horses that are only a little lame," said Donald Oge. "A day's rest would cure them. And it is disgraceful that we should move so fast with the enemy behind us. The whole matter has the appearance of flight and that is something that does not sit well with me at all."

"It is intended to have the appearance of flight, Donald Oge," said Peter. "We draw Tarleton on faster and faster and further away from Cornwallis. When we get him so far away that he cannot rejoin Cornwallis in a hurry, then we will turn on him and that will be at the Cowpens."

"I do not like this method of fighting at all," said Donald Oge. "It is what women would do or the Sassenachs. It is not a man's way—to run from his enemy."

"You can fight by running as well as by advancing on the enemy," said Peter. "And as for a real fight, you will have a belly full of that in a little while."

"If there is to be a charge made against the Redcoats," said Donald Oge, "I would ask the honor of leading it as a Farqueson."

Peter gave him a hard look.

"Well," said Donald Oge. "I have not much practice in being this new kind of a soldier that you want me to be, who fights according to orders and without any regard for the honor of himself and his people. So you must be patient with me until I learn the new way. If a charge is made and you ask the Frasers to lead it, I will abide by it. But I will not love you the more for it."

"I do not care if you love me or not," said Peter, "so long as you obey my orders."

"You are a very hard man to be agreeable with," said Donald Oge. "I think it is because you have too much English blood. You are altogether too level-headed and that is what is hard to put up with in you. By God, if you would do something wrong, it would give me a chance to forgive you and then we would be better friends. But you are always right and that is something more than a man can bear."

For a moment Peter was reminded of Peace of God Manly and his prayer that he, Peter, should be smitten down in his pride, so as to be humbled. He wondered whether he was indeed becoming too sure and smug with himself, but he put the thought aside. He had done very well and was respected by men like Nollichucky Jack and Morgan and Greene. He had even had a personal interview with General Washington and that interview might have been a factor in the replacement of Gates by General Greene. There was hardly a man in his command who was not older than he, and he alone had been able to weld them together into the fighting force known as Treegate's Raiders. He had, after all, a right to be proud of his achievements and his reputation. To be humble would be hypocritical for he did not feel humble.

"It is not my part as a leader to be wrong," Peter said to Donald Oge who grunted and went off.

The next day McClintock was told to take a party of ten men and ride back until he made contact with Tarleton and then return and report how far away Tarleton was. McClintock returned with the news that Tarleton was scarcely fifteen miles in the rear and his men in excellent condition despite the weather. They had plenty of baggage and horses and tents.

"It is a pretty sight to see them," said McClintock. "They are marching in fine order with a drummer to beat the time for them despite the rain and their flags flying as brave as you could please."

He turned to Donald Oge. "There is a Highland regiment with them and they are wearing the Fraser tartan," he said.

"It is small help we can expect from the Frasers among us then," he said, "for they will not fire on their own blood."

The remark angered Peter and because he was angry he spoke savagely and without thinking.

"You fired on your own blood, did you not, Donald Oge?" he asked. Donald Oge gave him an agonized look and went off without a word. Peter was immediately repentant and called out to him but Donald Oge did not turn. Peter knew he should have gone after the mountaineer and said how bitterly he regretted his words, but a stubborn pride prevented him and he stayed where he was.

McClintock looked at Peter and then hung his head. "Go with him if you want," said Peter bitterly. But McClintock stayed where he was.

"Why did I say such a thing to him?" Peter asked himself. "He killed his own brother to save my life, and I threw it in his face."

He could find no answer that satisfied him and turned in for the night, feeling miserable.

*14* ☆

Banastre Tarleton was in the highest of spirits. He was a man with such an appetite for victory that he was incapable of recognizing when he had suffered defeat. Indeed his self-assurance and spirit were such that he considered himself as a second Alexander, going from triumph to triumph with never a check to his list of victories. He was all full of fire and dash and show and loved a military display so that he dressed his cavalrymen in the gaudy uniform of dragoons, with plumed helmets of brass upon their heads and frogging of gold lace on their jackets. The cost he defrayed from his own pocket and thought it little when he reviewed his handsome company of horsemen.

Nor was his pride in himself and his achievements

without some justification. In any army whose top leaders were cautious plodders such as Clinton and Cornwallis and Rawlton, Tarleton was a man of fire and of
speed. He had many times routed bands of Continental
irregulars and militia whom he referred to as "damned
rebels" as if the two words were one. He moved fast,
struck hard and left terror behind him. Rumor had it
that since the start of the war in the colonies he had
hung several hundred men out of hand, for rebellion
against their sovereign lord the King. And if Tarleton
heard of this rumor he did not deny it, for he viewed
hanging as the only cure for "damned rebels," sniffed
at those among his fellow officers who spoke of clem-
ency and reconciliation, and firmly believed that the
King's rule in the American colonies might be restored
and maintained only after the American rebels had
been cowed into submission.

At his officer's mess at headquarters or in the field, he
toasted the King every night in claret brought over
from England, discussed fox hunting, horses, rebellion
and hanging and looked to the day when he might perhaps obtain a seat in the House of Lords as a result of
his services to the crown in subduing the American rebellion.

This then was the man Cornwallis detached with a
force of over a thousand men to overtake and exterminate the cornered Daniel Morgan at Cowpens; and who
could look to the morrow to smashing Morgan's army
completely.

It would have been ridiculous to suggest that Tarleton could not achieve this. Every aspect of the situation favored him. For one thing, Morgan's force consisted largely of militia and Tarleton well knew that the American militia had not sufficient discipline to withstand a charge delivered by British regulars. For another, Morgan had chosen what must surely be the poorest ground on which to make a stand. He was encamped on a slight rise with a river protecting his left flank. But that same river curved around to the rear of Morgan's army, making it impossible for him to retreat. He had put himself into a position where he must stand and fight it out and this was precisely what Tarleton hoped for.

Again, Tarleton had an excellent body of men under his command—magnificent troops who were already veterans of several years' campaigning in the American colonies. There were five hundred of his own Legion, horse and foot—men whose very name struck terror into the hearts of the colonists. Then there was a battalion of the Royal Fusiliers and another of the 71st Highland Regiment, the "Fighting Frasers" as they were known; a company of the 17th Light Dragoons and another of the Royal Artillery. Added to this were a number of Tory militia making a total force of eleven hundred men, fully armed, fully clothed, fully fed and fully confident.

Morgan was in disorder with his back to the wall, having been in full retreat for several days. Plainly there lay ahead for General Banastre Tarleton another of those swift brilliant victories on which he thrived and which would take him one step nearer to that seat in the House of Lords which would certainly be his reward at the end of the war.

"Gentlemen," he said, rising to propose a toast for his fellow officers on the evening before battle, "let us drink to the restoration of His Majesty's rule in these colonies and the extermination of his enemies in the affair that lies before us tomorrow."

The toast was drunk in high spirits and certainty of victory.

Meanwhile, in the American camp that evening, the morale of the men was not so high. To be sure Morgan had been reinforced by the arrival of Brigadier General Andrew Pickens with seventy riflemen from North Carolina. But the militia were nervous and did not like the field picked for battle for the precise reason that no avenue of retreat was offered. They must stand and fight and the man they must stand against was the devil Tarleton who offered no quarter to men who had surrendered, but killed them regardless.

The militia conferred in undertones over their campfires the evening before battle and generally agreed that they had been led into an untenable position and would be slaughtered on the following day. Some of their anxiety spread to the irregulars who, although more accustomed to action, still did not like a battleground from which there was no avenue of retreat. Their method was to strike hard and fast and then get away to strike again. But now they must strike hard and remain where they were to deal with the counterblow from British regulars with their accursed bayonets.

Morgan held a brief council of war before dinner that night. It was not a council in which he asked the opinion of his officers on what was best to do. It was a council rather in which he gathered them together to tell them what he was about to do and made it plain that he wanted no suggestions. Because he was such a magnificent soldier they listened without demur. But the plan he laid before them violated all the rules of strategy.

"We have two small hills and a thinly wooded plain before us," he said, "and it is as nice a piece of ground to fight on as a man could wish for. There is a river to our left which curves around behind us and cuts off retreat and there is another small stream to our right that will serve the same purpose, so we are boxed in and must fight it out. I came here to fight, gentlemen, and I do not want any retreating. It is a bad thing all together for a man to have one eye on the enemy and the other on an escape road behind him."

"But the militia . . ." said Pickens who knew the militia well.

"The militia will want to run when they see the Redcoats come down on them," said Morgan calmly. "And I do not blame them, because before I had any training in fighting, I wanted to run myself in such circumstances. Well, they will have my permission to run. Captain Treegate has suggested that they should fire two rounds and then quit the field and made the further suggestion that they be given permission to do so, which is what I intend. I will ask only this of the militia —that they stay steady enough to fire two rounds.

Then they may retreat behind the first of the hills with honor and sit around playing cards or doing whatever takes their fancy for the rest of the battle.

"However, to get off their two rounds with any effect at all they must be in clear sight of the enemy and so I will put them in the front line with the other troops and the irregulars on the hill a hundred and fifty yards behind them."

"Your untried men in the forefront of the battle and unsupported?" cried Pickens, aghast.

"Yes," said Morgan. "But they have only to fire two rounds and then they can skedaddle and I will give a medal to every man among them who wants it, for they will have served their purpose."

Pickens face was pale with horror. It was contrary to all the rules of warfare to put untried troops in the first line of battle. The bravest among them would run out of sheer nerves at the firing of the first shot. Their panic would encourage the enemy and demoralize the rest of the army. What Morgan proposed then was a plan not for victory but for defeat—indeed disaster, and Pickens plainly stated that he thought this was so.

"I'm obliged to you for your views, look you," said Morgan. "But the Old Wagoner will crack his whip over the backs of the Redcoats tomorrow and with the very plan he has laid before you." The "Old Wagoner" was the name Morgan was known by among the men, referring to the days when he had been a drover, taking freight wagons into the interior of the country in a roadless wilderness. He delighted in the name and he used it now with a special pleasure, remembering perhaps the time when he had been trussed to a wagon wheel by the British and flogged until his back was a tangle of bloodied flesh. "Aye," he said, "I'll crack my whip and it is they who will do the screaming and beseech me to let up." There was a savage look in his dark eyes for a moment. Then he turned to Peter.

"I want you to pick a hundred of the best riflemen we have, Captain Treegate," he said, "and form a skirmish line about fifty yards ahead of the militia. When the British advance, let them come to within fifty yards and then open fire. Shoot for the men with the epaulettes. One officer is worth twenty infantrymen for the infantrymen are lost without their officers. They can take orders but they cannot think for themselves, that being the manner of their training. Get off as many rounds as you can, each man picking his target and taking his time. Then retreat back to the militia line, stay there to give them courage until they have got off their two rounds. When they have withdrawn to the right, you can fall back to the forces behind you."

Peter nodded. Morgan gave Peter a shrewd look. "I have heard that there is some bad blood between your raiders and yourself," he said. "Don't ask who told me. The Old Wagoner listens to every creak of the wheel. What is it about?"

"It's their damnable clannish spirit," said Peter with more heat than he had intended. "There is a regiment of Frasers among the British and the Farquesons among my men say that those of the Fraser clan will not fight against their kin on the British side. I've been bothered with this same curse ever since I left the mountains with them."

"I will give you a word of advice," said Morgan, "and then pass on to other things. You cannot fight pride with pride. What conquers pride is humility for in the face of the humble the proud are without a word. So it was with Christ when He was on the face of this earth and that is one great lesson that can be learned from Him. If then there is any matter of pride on your part that vexes your men, mend it yourself. If you have done any one of them a wrong, see that you ask his forgiveness and he will think the more of you."

Peter was surprised to hear the great Daniel Morgan talking in a strain more suited to Peace of God Manly. He shrugged the admonition aside. He was not, he told himself, a proud man and though he had hurt Donald Oge Farqueson it had been under provocation and in anger and Donald Oge should realize this. He decided he would tell him he was sorry. But he would not go out of his way to do so.

Meanwhile Morgan went ahead laying out his plan of battle. Peter, busy with his own thoughts, did not get all the details. But matters were clear in his mind. There would be a picket or skirmish line of his own raiders. Behind that the militia. Behind them the troops and irregulars. And behind them, hidden from the enemy by a hill, the cavalry who would charge into action on Morgan's orders only. When the conference broke up, Peter was about to leave to find McClintock and Donald Oge and tell them to pick the men for the skirmish line. But Morgan beckoned to Peter to come with him.

Peter thought he was going to get another lecture but instead Morgan led him to the place where the militiamen were camped and cooking their dinners in little groups over a hundred small fires. He visited each group, clapping the men on the back, joking with them about their food, entertaining them with little anecdotes of his days in the wilderness. He had the knack of making each man feel that he was a personal friend and confidant of Daniel Morgan. They were uneasy when he came but they were laughing when he left. He explained to every group exactly what his plan of battle was and what part the militia would play.

"Two rounds, boys," he said. "Two rounds is all I ask of you and then you can wander off and write to your wives and sweethearts for the day will be won. And let me tell you this. It will be won because of the militia— because of those two rounds that you're going to fire into them as they come down on you for the sake of the Old Wagoner."

"We'll stay as long as you want, Dan, and fire twenty rounds if that is what is needed."

"Aye, I know ye would," said Morgan. "But don't be greedy for all the glory. Give the others a little piece of it. But I'll tell you this, solemn as a judge, that the battle will be won because of you boys standing there and firing those two rounds for me."

So he went tirelessly from group to group until there was not one man of the militia but could say he had spoken personally with Dan Morgan that night on the evening of battle. Young and old he made them his men, giving them courage and confidence, making them feel a zest for the trial ahead. When he was done their fears were gone. They were ready for the Red-coats and the dreaded dragoons of Tarleton.

*15* ☆

There was a touch of frost in the air the morning of the British attack at Cowpens, and the men in the American lines who had been up before dawn to take their positions were shivering before the sun came up—a huge red ball—in the east. There was no warmth in the sun but the increase of light seemed to diminish the cold though it threw stark shadows on their bearded faces and made of the tangle of grass and scrub before them a landscape uncommonly like a neglected graveyard.

The militia were in line with the regulars behind them. And before the militia were Treegate's Raiders, each man fifteen feet from his neighbor so that in the rank grass each was in a little world of his own without help from his fellows and depending for his safety entirely on his own courage and skill. Peter had picked the best of the riflemen—men who could hit a target dead center at a hundred and fifty paces with a heavy cross wind. But he sensed about them a certain coldness toward him and knew that this was because of the remark he had made to Donald Oge about the killing of his brother.

He had sought Donald Oge intending to apologize and ask forgiveness, but the man's attitude had been distant and haughty and he had avoided meeting Peter except in the presence of others. Peter could not bring himself to apologize with others around and so the matter stood—the men cold to their leader rather than loyal, resentful of him because he was not one of them and because, despite all the complicated feuds among them, that leader had hurt one of their fellows whom they held in high regard.

The only exception was big McClintock. Doggedly loyal to Peter, he did his best to warm the feelings of the men. But he was a man clumsy with words and without agility in persuasion. Perhaps of them all McClintock suffered the most, torn between the old loyalties and a reverence bordering on worship for his young captain.

The British attack came shortly after sunrise. Tarleton himself swept onto the field with a company of his flashily dressed dragoons. First there was a flourish of bugles playing a fox hunting snatch and then out of the blue mist to the south came Tarleton and perhaps twenty men, at full gallop thundering down on the

American lines. He reined in out of rifle shot, stood up in his stirrups and surveyed the American position ahead of him. What he saw—two lines of the enemy with the militia in the front line—pleased him enormously.

"By God," he said to an aide, "Morgan is a bigger fool than I took him for. He has trapped himself. There's the river on his flank and behind him and over to his right another stream. He can't retreat and we can smash him with one charge of cavalry."

He had been surveying the American lines through a collapsible telescope which fitted snugly into a leather cylinder on his saddle. He handed the telescope to his aide who surveyed the American position and gave it back dubiously.

"Morgan's no fool," said the aide slowly. "There must be something more in their battle plan than we can see."

"My good friend," said Tarleton, "since the start of this wretched revolution, the whole British command from Clinton down has been expecting strength in the enemy that just isn't there. You see before you the whole American position. Do not look for phantoms to fight. Morgan is in full retreat. We've been following him for days and seen his baggage strewn along the route. He's at bay now and one cavalry charge with sabers will cut his wretched army to pieces. After that, the bayonet and the hangman's rope can finish the work."

This was the sole council of war of the impetuous and victorious Tarleton whose name alone was worth a regiment because of the terror it struck into the hearts of the enemy. He wheeled about and went back to meet his own army, coming up towards Cowpens and but a mile off. He had quickly given his orders. The dragoons would charge immediately. The infantry would form a line of battle fronting the enemy, with their small cannon placed in the center and on the two wings. The Highlanders would be on the right, facing the American left, and the Fusiliers on the left wing. As soon as the dragoons had smashed into the American lines and thrown them into confusion, they would withdraw; the cannon would open fire and the infantry advance with the bayonet to finish up the work.

Tarleton was so impatient to start that he was hardly prepared to wait until the infantry were in position. He fumed and fretted while the Redcoats formed off in companies, marched to their position and then formed their battle lines—all done with great nicety to drum rolls, bugle flourishes and sharp commands from their officers.

The Americans watched this with growing admiration and awe. They had no drill to match this careful and deliberate preparation for battle. Morgan went along the line of the militia with Pickens. He knew that the militia were likely to be overawed and demoralized by the British preparations—the drum rolls, the shrilling of fifes, the precise wheeling of company after company into line of battle. He had a stub of clay pipe in his mouth and his rifle slung over his shoulder, presenting a comfortable contrast to the frightful and dreaded machine of war which was being assembled scarcely half a mile away.

"All according to plan, boys," he said. "Couldn't be better if I'd ordered it myself. See how nice they pack themselves together for those two volleys you are going to give them for me. Why the first volley will bring down half and the next will take care of the rest of them. Only fire low for me boys. Hit 'em in the bellies. You there now, show me how you will do it."

The man he spoke to was a portly merchant from Camden. His big jowls were white with apprehension and his hands trembled on his musket. He gave a sickly grin and aimed the musket in the general direction of the British line. But he was trembling so much that it was plain his shot would go wild when it was fired. Morgan put a big hand on his shoulder.

"That's as good as I've seen from a regular," he said. "There's men in the Continental Line could take a lesson from you. Just keep the barrel down and don't mind the shakes. Everybody gets them. Take your ease and fire slow and in two rounds it will all be done. Six minutes at the most and we've won the day." The man nodded, too overcome to speak. Then he looked into Morgan's hard weathered face and mumbled, "I'm sorry I've got the shakes. But I'll do what I can."

"Of course you will," said Morgan. "Better men I've never had to my back. The Old Wagoner won't forget a one of you." So he went all along the line of the militia leaving comfort and courage behind him, and telling the men that when Treegate's Raiders fell back, it was not a retreat but part of the plan and they were to open their ranks and receive them.

"Two volleys," he kept saying. "Two volleys." And he made it sound like such a little thing that the fear left them and they looked to their priming and promised they'd shoot low and stand until told to move off.

Among Treegate's Raiders meanwhile there was great excitement when the Highlanders in the British line came into place. They were led into the line by their pipers playing the "Pibroch of Donald Dhu"— the "War Song of Donald the Black." The tartan of their kilts—a red ground with green and blue overcrossings—flashed bravely in the sun and one of the Frasers in Peter's line stood up and shouted in Gaelic "Go to the other end! Go to the other end! There are Frasers of your own clan here against you."

There was no reply to this and indeed no immediate sign that the words were heard. But when the Highlanders were in position their pipers changed briefly from a war song to the "Lament for the Fraser Men"—a salute to those of the clan who were opposed to them and about to die. Peter moving from man to man along his thin picket line came upon one of the Frasers who turned on him fiercely. "Why must I kill my own blood?" he demanded.

"For liberty," said Peter quietly.

"We had liberty enough in the old days in the clan," was the reply.

"The clans are gone," said Peter. "The chief of the Frasers now is King George of England and it is his money the Frasers take to fight this day."

"God's curse on the day the clans were broken," said the man quietly. "May there be no rest for those that broke them." Then he cocked his rifle and rubbed the flint with his thumb to see that it was dry and would fire well. Peter came next on Donald Oge who eyed him stonily. The hate in the man's eyes cut off the apology Peter wanted to make. He went by him in silence and then satisfied that all his men were in position, took his own place thirty feet in front of his line, utterly alone with the enemy ahead and his own men, indifferent to whether he lived or died, behind.

Before the last of the British lines had been formed, Tarleton could contain his impatience no longer. He had assembled his dragoons behind the line and now with a flourish of bugles led them around to the left flank where there was open ground over which they could charge. He did not even bother to form them into companies but rose in his stirrups, waved his naked saber and pointed directly at the center of the American line. The bugles sounded the full charge and the whole body of splendidly equipped and mounted men flung themselves at the American center, the ground shaking under the drumming of the horses' hooves and the air rent by the roars of the dragoons. Nearer and nearer they thundered until Peter was able to see the gold frogging on the jackets of individual troopers.

Peter rose in the long grass to a kneeling position and his men behind him did the same. The sight of the riflemen rising as it were from the ground sent a shock through the dragoons and their cheering died for a moment. Then there was a crackle of rifle fire and sixty of them tumbled without a word off their horses to be trampled under the feet of the animals behind. The charge slowed for a fraction of a second and there was a cheer from the militia. Then the dragoons regained their stride and came on again.

Only half of Peter's men had fired. The other half now selected their targets, gave a volley, and another score of dragoons went down. There was now no time to reload. The horsemen were within a hundred yards, so Peter's men, crouching low, slipped quickly back to the militia line and reloaded there.

The dragoons, seeing the riflemen run, cheered and broke up to saber individual men, urging their horses forward. Now came the first of those precious volleys from the militia for which Morgan had worked so hard. It erupted in a disorderly cracking sound all along the militia line. Jets of yellow flame flickered wickedly from one end of the line to the other, followed by a billowing cloud of white smoke. The charge of the dragoons was stopped as if the riders had come up against an invisible wall. Men and horses were flung to the ground as if they had been hit from above by invisible hammers. When the smoke cleared away the charge was over. A few horsemen milled around for a moment, uncertain what to do, and then took flight and headed back for their own lines over a field now littered with dead and wounded men and animals.

The militia seeing this cheered themselves hoarse and their officers were hard put to get them to reload.

The British infantry had watched all this impassively, standing to arms. When the remainder of Tarleton's men came back, they opened their lines to let them through and then closed again. The drums rolled. The fifes shrilled. Then came the order "Mount bayonets." The bayonets flashed briefly in little arcs in the sun as they were pulled from their scabbards and mounted on the ends of the muskets. The cheering in the ranks of the American militia died away. The next order was "The line will advance with the bayonet," clearly heard in the American lines. There was a ruffling of drums and the Redcoats stepped off, maintaining perfect formation, as the drummer boys at the end of each company beat time for the step.

Nearer and nearer they came and the American militia watching them looked anxiously at each other and gripped their muskets harder. The heavy-set merchant from Camden to whom Morgan had spoken was trembling so badly that his musket nearly fell from his hands. Peter had entered the line beside him and he felt sorry for the man. He was kneeling but his whole frame was shaking with nerves.

"Lie down," said Peter, "and just reckon it target practice. You'll be all right."

"I'm scared," said the man.

"So are they," said Peter. "Only they are trained not to show it. Think how they must feel marching down on us and waiting for a volley at any moment."

The merchant became calmer. Still the British line advanced to the tapping of the drums, their blade leggings swishing through the long grass. The little cannon fired a few rounds over their heads, the balls plumping into the American works but with little harm. Then, to a flourish of bugles, the Redcoats halted. The distance was only fifty yards. They were in two rows and the first row squatted down as one man and brought their muskets level to present a thicket of barrels aimed at the militia. This was the moment for which Morgan had been waiting. He shouted the order to the militia to give their second volley.

It roared out like the first—a deafening ripping explosion that burst in flame and smoke from one end of the militia line to the other. The Redcoats toppled to the ground like poppies before the scythe. Their line was ripped into shreds by the hail of bullets that was flung upon them. When the smoke of the discharge cleared a third of them were prostrate on the ground.

But they did not retreat. They closed ranks and fired their own volley.

Then they came on again—with the bayonet.

## *16* ☆

Across the narrowing strip of ground, strewn with rank brown grass and thickets of small brush, which separated the American lines from the advancing British, there now spread a pall of white gunsmoke. It was thick and heavy and lay upon the ground so that the British lines seemed to be wading through it, with only their shoulders visible above this ocean of smoke. They came on steadily, still to the beat of the drum. The drummer boys increased the rhythm of the beat for it was time now for the Redcoats to break from their walk into a trot and soon they would be at the full charge and fling themselves upon the American lines.

The militia had now fired their two volleys. Some

of them reloaded, uncertain in their excitement how many volleys they had fired. Others just stared, appalled at the sight of the advancing lines of the enemy, and moved back slowly on the regulars behind them. Then Pickens called on them to stand firm and a moment later gave the order to the militia to file off to the right.

To their credit, they did not run. They marched off to circle to the right behind the regulars, their part of the work done as had been agreed with Morgan the night before. But some companies lagging behind the others, or delayed by an obstacle, or misunderstanding the order to withdraw, were left. These, seeing their fellows depart, broke into a run to catch up with them.

The British took the withdrawal of the militia for retreat and gave a loud yell. They broke immediately into a trot and then into a lumbering run, the gunsmoke swirling around them and the tips of their bayonets gleaming above it. They came on in this manner perhaps twenty paces when the line of regulars and raiders which had been drawn up behind the militia opened fire. The volley came at point-blank range and the effect was appalling. Men shot in mid-stride leaped into the air like hooked trout and tumbled to the ground. Others crashed forward or tumbled back, twisting around, or stood for one stunned moment before crumbling to the ground. The cheers of the charge changed to screams of pain. The beat of the drums ceased and the British advance was stopped.

For one terrible minute there was nothing to be heard but the shouts and groans and curses of the wounded men. Then, from the British right came the skirling of pipes and the Highland regiment, which had also withstood three volleys of fire at point-blank range, plunged headlong behind the pipers into the American line.

They were met by the American forces and the men of Treegate's Raiders who had now dropped back to the last line of defense.

The Highlanders had thrown aside their rifles for their love was cold steel rather than hot lead. They charged with dirk, sword and claymore, and were met, steel to steel and body to body by the knives and bayonets of the Americans. A murderous hand-to-hand combat ensued in which Peter Treegate, standing head and shoulders above his fellows, fought like a Samson.

Near him was McClintock and to his left Donald Oge Farqueson and these three, using hunting knives and clubbed rifles, cleared an area for themselves in the press of the Highlanders. Peter saw some of his own men who were Frasers engaged in the combat, locked in a death struggle with their own kin. No quarter was asked or given and gradually the Highlanders were driven back. They retreated only a little way and then forming again, charged once more. This time they were met with rifle fire and lost a third of their number. Still they charged again and the very fury of their assault drove the American line back at that point.

Meanwhile Tarleton had been trying to lead the survivors of his dragoons in another charge. But they flatly refused to follow him. Furious, Tarleton rallied the British infantry and led them to the opposite end of the American line from that at which the highlanders were engaged. But Morgan had seen and anticipated the move. He called on his regulars to protect their flank by moving to make a right angle with their main line. But it was the militia who came to the rescue.

They had moved to the rear as ordered but now, without any command, they went into the battle again, moving up company by company like so many veterans. They were in position when Tarleton led his last desperate charge. They met him with a volley of fire and then, led by Pickens, and with small swords strapped to their musket barrels, they charged into the mass of the Redcoats.

The Redcoats broke and tried to rally once more. But Morgan called on his small reserve of cavalry, hidden far behind the slight hill to the rear. Out they streamed, sabers flashing in the wintry sun, smashed through the British line, turned and smashed it again, until soon the line was gone and there was nothing but huddled groups of soldiers, their muskets thrown aside and their arms raised in surrender.

The battle was over and won. Even the highlanders withdrew, leaving half their number on the field, the red of their tartans now darkened with their blood.

Donald Oge, seeing the withdrawal, looked over to where the small British cannon had been placed. They were still there and the gunners were still serving their pieces though completely unsupported by infantry.

"Follow me, the Farquesons," he cried and dashed with perhaps twenty men behind him toward the guns. He was fascinated by the cannon and determined to capture one which would, in his view, make him as good a man as his father.

Peter shouted to the men to stay but he had lost control of them. They streamed after Donald Oge and hurled themselves on the gunners. The gunners did not surrender and were killed to the last man. Donald Oge captured a bewildered horse which stood beside the dead body of its rider and, with the help of two men, flung a small "grasshopper" cannon on its back and brought it to the American lines in triumph.

When he got there McClintock came running to him. "Shame on you, Donald Oge, that you left your leader for the second time."

"I wanted the cannon," said the other. "And anyway the day was won. Where is he?"

"He is a prisoner," said McClintock. "He was taken by three horsemen who came down on him, picking him out from all the other men. He was alone and they clubbed him to the ground and took him off. I was too far off to help."

Donald Oge considered this for a while but shrugged and said nothing.

"It is in your place to rescue him," stormed McClintock.

"Whatever debt I owed him I paid with the death of my brother," said Donald Oge. "I saved his life once and he gave me no thanks for it but threw it in my face."

"The fault was not all his," said McClintock. "There was provocation on your side and you will acknowledge it if you are a gentleman."

"I will be the best judge of that," said Donald Oge. "The man is all discipline and has no love in him. Well, let his discipline stand him in good stead now—or later when he has a noose around his neck. I would be glad to know whether he flinches at the touch of the rope."

McClintock was not to be put off. "It is in your place to rescue Captain Treegate," he said. "There will be shame on you for all time if you leave him to be hung."

Donald Oge gave him a hard look and then said, "Very well. But I will do it in my own way and in my own time. Now get the men together and find out how many are dead and how many wounded. And see to it that nobody steals this cannon which I captured myself from the enemy, for I intend to take it back to the valley and set it up before my father's house."

With that McClintock had to be content.

Tarleton meanwhile had barely escaped from the field of Cowpens. The man whose career had been a progression of victories, whose very name was a weapon because of the terror it conveyed, had now suffered a defeat which could be construed in no other way. His whole command was gone. There remained but the tatters of the army which that morning he had led so confidently into battle. He assembled what remained of his force, and without staying to collect the wounded, fled headlong to join up with his commander-in-chief, Lord Cornwallis, whose army lay to the east and south of Cowpens and was marching in that direction. A mud besplattered rider informed Cornwallis of the Cowpens disaster and a few hours later Tarleton himself arrived to give the story of the defeat.

With his eyes on the seat in the House of Lords which he had always coveted, Tarleton tried to make light of the matter, urging that he had inflicted a crippling blow on Morgan's command and arguing that if Cornwallis would immediately march on Morgan, who lay but a day away, he could overwhelm him, delivering a death blow to an army already grievously wounded by Tarleton.

Cornwallis listened in silence. The more Tarleton talked, the more sure of himself he became, until when he had finished his explanation, there was a note almost of triumph in his voice. Tarleton had in fact begun to believe that, heavily as he had been mangled himself, Morgan's men had been mangled more. If an outright victory were not now achieved, the fault would lie not with Banastre Tarleton but with Lord Cornwallis.

"Why," said Tarleton, as he concluded, "in leaving the field we even managed to capture one of the partisan leaders. His men had run from him, leaving him all alone."

"Whom did you capture?" asked Cornwallis, with a touch of sarcasm in his tone. "Morgan?"

"No," replied Tarleton. "Treegate. The same Treegate whose raiders bedevilled Ferguson into the death-trap of King's Mountain."

"What do you propose to do with him?" asked Cornwallis.

"Hang him," said Tarleton.

"On what charge?" asked Cornwallis.

"The usual ones," replied Tarleton. "Incitement to

rebellion and the murder of troops engaged in the service of His Majesty. I assure you, My Lord, the hanging will have the most salutory effect upon the population. They have been much encouraged in their rebellious attitude by the disaster of Ferguson. Today's engagement will make them more mutinous. But if they find that this fellow Treegate has been hung forthwith, they will have second thoughts about taking up arms against their king."

"Tarleton," said Cornwallis soberly, "you are a brilliant officer and none can deny your courage. You lack only one quality to make you one of the greatest ornaments of His Majesty's forces."

"And what is that, My Lord?" asked Tarleton.

"You are completely incapable of distinguishing fact from fiction," said Cornwallis soberly. "You have been speaking to me as if this affair at Cowpens were almost a victory with the final blow waiting to be struck by me. The fact is that you were completely defeated by an inferior force and have lost the greater part of your command. To be sure I must strike and strike fast. But I strike not to follow up an advantage gained by you but to overcome, if possible, a terrible blow suffered by your command.

"Again you talk about these Americans as rebels who have mutinied against their king. That is a fiction, sir, a plain fiction, used to justify hanging for the purposes of terror. The fact is that the Americans have some years ago—four years ago to be exact—solemnly foresworn, before the nations of the world, all allegiance to the king and cut all ties with the British

throne. So we are engaged at the moment not in sup-
pressing a rebellion, but in an attempt at conquest of a
people determined to rule themselves.

"For public purposes we talk of this as a rebellion.
But it would be better for you and me if we faced the
facts and recognized that we are engaged in conquest."

"I had not thought to hear you talk so perilously
close to treason," said Tarleton, white with anger.

Cornwallis flushed. "I have given long service to the
King," he said. "Longer than you, Tarleton, risking my
life, my reputation and my fortune in the defense of
the throne. I shall continue to do so. You may retract
your remark about treason as unfitting in a gentleman."

Tarleton hesitated and then surrendered. "I do retract it, My Lord," he said. "I spoke in anger."

"The incident is forgotten," said Cornwallis.

"Your orders, My Lord?" said Tarleton.

"Orders?" said Cornwallis as if the word puzzled
him. He seemed very weary. "Orders. We break camp at
dawn, burn the baggage, the tents and surplus stores
and set out in pursuit of Morgan. He must be caught
and smashed or the game is lost."

There was a map on the camp table before him and
he pointed to it. "Morgan may remain where he is at
Cowpens, celebrating his victory or resting from it," he
said. "I hope he does. Or he may try to link with General Greene. Whatever he does we must catch and destroy him or we lose the Carolinas and Georgia and
Virginia as well. We cannot afford that loss."

His eyes moved eastward across the map, studying
the rivers. Such strange names—Catawba, Peedee, Eno-

ree, Santee. They spoke of the wilderness in all its desolation. Then he caught sight of a name on the map that brought a smile to his lips.

"Yorktown," he said aloud. "Yorktown. How good to find an English sounding name in this terrible country."

# *17* ☆

The pursuit was on now, the desperate chase of the American forces by Cornwallis. Neither commander was in any doubt of the issues at stake in this. General Greene dared not be caught for that would mean a general engagement with a superior army. Win or lose, the casualties would be so heavy that there would be no Continental force worth talking about in the southern colonies. He must flee northward and crossing the Dan, get into Virginia where he could expect reinforcements, or at least make a stand with that broad river before him as a bulwark.

Cornwallis on the other hand knew he must catch Morgan and Greene, and defeat them utterly. If he did not do so, he would lose control of the Carolinas and

Georgia, for the people could not be brought into subjection while Greene's army still existed.

He struck first toward Morgan who he hoped was still in the vicinity of Cowpens. But the "Old Wagoner" had gone. He had stayed on the field of his triumph long enough only to bury the dead and put the wounded under the care of a surgeon. Then he called his army on parade and thanked them for the victory they had won. He particularly praised the militia for standing so firm, giving him his two volleys and then rallying again. And seeing in the ranks that same merchant from Camden who had trembled so he shook his hand, gave him a pistol and said, "Look you, I wish I had two thousand fellows of your kind that tremble so much and fight so well. For it seems to me that a little shaking is the sign of a good fighter."

Then he raised his voice to address the whole body of his men. In private conversation he could talk quietly. But before a multitude he had a trail boss' voice and it was said he could be heard half a mile above a gale of wind.

"Now my good friends," he roared. "We must skedaddle. We must get out of here fast and join General Greene. No shame to it. Cornwallis is scarcely twenty-five miles from here and there're rivers to be crossed and all of them in flood. We beat them in a fight and now we're going to beat them in a footrace. Let each man help his neighbor and throw away what he doesn't need. But hold on to your rifles and bullet pouches and powder horns. A man can go three days without food in this country but not one minute without a firearm."

Half an hour later the race was on. The south fork of the Catawba was crossed that night and the north fork, terribly swollen by rains in the mountains, a day later. When Cornwallis arrived at Cowpens, Morgan had already crossed two rivers and was still plunging on in a desperate race to link with Greene. Cornwallis had destroyed the greater part of his baggage before setting out in pursuit. He now destroyed the rest, even staving in the puncheons of rum carried for the troops. The soldiers sadly watched the liquor poured onto the sullen, muddy ground. It was followed by Cornwallis' own personal store of wine. And to this was added Tarleton's private stock in which he had been wont each night to toast the King.

Then with only four wagons for ambulances and with each man carrying his own stores in his haversack, Cornwallis took up the pursuit again. Morgan, Cornwallis learned at the south fork of the Catawba, was two days ahead of him and moving fast. Very well, the British must move faster. They would march day and night, resting only briefly. Men who dropped behind would be at the mercy of the people of the countryside. When this was learned there were few who dropped out, the temper of the people being ugly against the British.

In one of the ambulances lay Peter Treegate. Clubbed from behind by a horseman in the very moment of victory at Cowpens, Tarleton had ordered that he be taken along. Now he lay in the wagon bound hand and foot, jolted from side to side and incapable of any movement to protect himself.

He remained in this condition for two days during which time he saw no one and received neither food nor water. On the evening of the third day, when Tarleton's men, who were bringing up the rear with the ambulances, were resting briefly, a guard came, cut the thongs that bound Peter's feet and tumbled him out of the wagon. He could not get up from the ground and finally had to be dragged upright by two guards who hauled him off to a tent inside which Tarleton sat. The guards released Peter and he slumped to the ground, still too weak to stand. Tarleton laughed.

"They are not so tough after all, these fearless partisan leaders and rebels," said Tarleton to one of the other officers with him. "One knock on the head and he is as weak as a baby. Well, my friend, you will have little use for your legs in future for you are to be hung by your neck until you are dead—and that in short order."

Peter said nothing. His head was swimming and his mind fuzzy. He caught only snatches of what was being said. A soldier threw a bucket of water over him and the shock of it helped to clear Peter's mind.

"Do you hear me, sirrah?" said Tarleton. "You are to be hanged as a damned murderer and rebel."

Peter nodded. There was much he wanted to say but his mind was so confused that he could not find the necessary words. He kept thinking of the old woman in the Farqueson's valley who had warned him to beware of the hangman's rope. It all seemed completely logical to him. The woman had warned him he was to be hanged and now Tarleton was telling him that this would be done. All he could do was accept his fate.

"Is he conscious?" asked Tarleton of one of the guards.

The guard seized Peter by his long hair and pulled his head back and peered into his face. "Yes, sir," he said. "He's conscious. But he hasn't got all his wits about him."

Tarleton nodded. "You are on trial for rebellion against your sovereign Lord King George the Third of England which constitutes the capital charge of treason," he said. "And you are further accused of raising a band of cutthroats and firing upon the King's troops and killing a number of them, which constitutes the capital charge of murder. Have you anything to say in your defense?"

Peter could hear the words quite distinctly, but they seemed to be coming to him in a dream. All he could think was that the woman had warned him he would be hung. That this was coming to pass neither appalled nor astonished him. It was something inevitable against which he could make no protest. There was a reason why he was to be hung. It had nothing to do with rebellion or what Tarleton was saying. He had done something terribly wrong, and hanging was the punishment. But he could not remember what it was he had done.

Tarleton was still talking, his words coming to Peter with a disembodied, dreamlike quality. Tarleton said something about "pride" and that word alone struck home. Pride. That was his fault. And then he remembered the terrible injury he had done Donald Oge and how he had been too proud to ask for forgiveness.

"Pride cometh before a fall." That was what Peace of God Manly had told him long long ago in a place that was a million miles away. Here was his fall and he was alone among his enemies like Samson among the Philistines. Peace of God had compared him to Samson, he remembered now. Either Peace of God or his daughter, Nancy. Yes. It was Nancy. She had spoken of him as Samson and he had been annoyed at the parallel and rejected it. He remembered her now for the first time since they had parted, with great longing. How frail and lovely she was and yet how strong in a quiet way. She was much stronger than he and yet he was the one who had prided himself on his strength. He had not known this but she had and gently warned him of it. How was it possible for a man to know so little about himself? He was a stranger to himself and only now, on the point of death, did he begin to know himself.

"Since you offer no defense for your actions and since they are indeed indefensible, the sentence of this court is that you be hung until dead," said Tarleton.

So that was it. He would not see Peace of God again, nor Nancy, to tell them that they had been right about his pride. He would like them to know that before he died he had been aware of the fault and repented it. But that was impossible. Tarleton was still speaking.

"Before sentence is carried out," he said, "I have

agreed to receive a petition on your behalf." His tone was bantering and he turned to one of the guards. "Bring in the petitioner," he said.

Peter raised his head. He was still thinking of Peace of God Manly, and he wondered whether the old sea captain had managed in some manner to get to this part of the wilderness to plead for him. But it was not Peace of God who now entered the tent but Donald Oge Farqueson. He had a piece of white cloth in his hand as a sign of truce and carried no weapons.

"Your name?" inquired Tarleton.

"Donald Oge Farqueson." He did not look at Peter who was staring at him.

"And your mission?"

"I have come to bargain for the life of that man there." He pointed to Peter.

"Bargain, by thunder," cried Tarleton. "My good friend, his life is forfeited a hundred times and there is no question of bargaining for it. But tell me, what did you propose to offer in trade?"

"A horse," said Donald Oge. "One horse."

"One horse?" cried Tarleton. "Come. Surely you were prepared to offer more for your leader."

"He is worth only one horse to me," said Donald Oge bitterly. "As I was to him. The horse is outside."

Peter now spoke for the first time. "I am to be hung," he said, soberly. "You will think I am afraid but I am not. I am glad you have come though, for I wanted to beg your forgiveness for what I said about your brother. When you killed him, you performed a greater sacrifice for liberty than anything I have ever done. I have talked about fighting for liberty and I have meant it. But you, with that one act, showed a greater devotion to liberty than anything I have shown in the whole course of the war."

Donald Oge now turned to Peter, his mouth twitching. "I loved my brother," he said. He spoke in Gaelic. "There is no love in you—only discipline. You have no love for any man."

"That is not true," said Peter. "I beg you to believe me. I would not lie to you in the face of death."

Donald Oge seemed uncertain what to say next. He made a move toward Peter but a guard came between the two of them.

"What more have you to say for yourself?" asked Tarleton who had been much puzzled by what had transpired.

"I will raise the price for this man's life," said Donald Oge. "I will give you three horses for him."

Tarleton's only reply was to laugh.

"I will give you three horses and myself for him," said Donald Oge.

"You cannot give me what is already mine," said Tarleton. "You are my prisoner at this very moment."

"But I have come to you under a flag of truce," said Donald Oge.

"There can be no truce with rebels any more than there can be a truce with criminals, for rebels are guilty of the most outrageous kind of crime—treason against their king." He nodded to the guards who closed round Donald Oge. Donald Oge looked at the guards evenly but made no attempt to escape. Then he spoke to Tarleton.

"I have a warning for you, my little bantam cock," he said. "And it is this. Do not ever surrender to any of us expecting quarter. For we will treat you as you have treated me. We will accept your surrender and wring your neck."

The two were taken outside but when they had gone a little distance from the tent, one of the guards went back to Tarleton to inquire what was to be done with Donald Oge.

"Hang him too," replied Tarleton. "He is as guilty as his fellow. And be quick about it. We are delayed long enough here and must catch up with the main body of the army."

Peter and Donald Oge were then taken to one of the wagons that served as an ambulance. They were made to stand on the wagon floor as halters were put around their necks. The wagon was then taken under a tree and the ends of the two ropes flung over a branch, the slack taken up, and secured there. The two men then had to stand on their toes not to be choked by the nooses around their necks. When the wagon was driven from under them, they would be hung.

The only illumination was provided by two dark lanterns. One of them stood on the floor of the wagon and the other had been taken up onto the limb of the tree by the soldier given the task of securing the ropes there. A soldier was standing near the wagon close to Donald Oge. He had a musket with him.

"If you will shoot me when the wagon is pulled away," said Donald Oge to the soldier, "you may have my hunting shirt. The others will respect the gift coming from a dying man. If you shoot me through the head the shirt will not be spoiled," he added simply. "It is a good shirt, scarcely a year old." The soldier consulted with a sergeant, nodded and backed off and raised his musket to have it ready.

"You should make a bargain too," said Donald Oge evenly to Peter. "It is not fit for a gentleman to die by hanging. There is a great deal of shame in it."

Peter turned to another soldier. "I do not care if I hang," he said. "That is what I was told would happen to me. But if you will ensure that my friend dies by musket shot, should the first soldier miss, you may have my hunting shirt." The man nodded and looked to the priming of his musket.

"Thank you," said Donald Oge. "I see now that you really do have a love for other men and it is not all discipline with you. I would be glad if we died friends."

"There is no quarrel between us now," said Peter. "We are friends and I am sorry about the past."

The time had now come to whip the horses so as to draw the wagon from under the two condemned men. The wagoner brought his whip down across their backs and the two horses lunged forward. But one lost its footing in the muddy ground so that although the wagon jerked forward, it went only a foot and then stopped. The effect was to cause the two men to stumble on the wagon bed but they regained their feet and Donald Oge shouted, "Shoot now and be done with it."

A musket shot rang out and Peter jerked his head away from Donald Oge and closed his eyes, thinking that his friend had been shot as he had asked. But then came several more reports. One of the horses went down, wounded and threshing in its harness. The wagon started to jerk backwards and forwards so that Peter was knocked off his feet and suspended by the rope around his neck which nearly strangled him. He could neither see nor understand what was happening, but opening his eyes briefly, saw in the muddy light of the dark lantern the ridiculous figure of Mr. Paddock. Mr. Paddock in his oversize hat and oversize boots was standing on tiptoes, a large knife in his hands, trying desperately to cut the rope around Peter's neck.

"What a terrible thing it is to be afraid," he cried. "All I have to do is cut this rope but at any moment I may be killed and I cannot get the knife to cut." So he went on, sawing away all the while but with no great result. Eventually whoever had cut down Donald Oge came to the assistance of the Mr. Paddock and Peter was freed. Musket balls were singing around them as they jumped off the wagon. Peter stumbled on a horse in the dark, flung Mr. Paddock on it and got up behind him. Donald Oge grabbed the horse's mane and they went off together in the darkness, Mr. Paddock pleading with them to go faster lest they be killed at any moment.

## 18 ☆

"It had been my fate for the past several years," said Mr. Paddock, "although a man of peace and pronounced timidity, to have been thrown into the very arms of Mars; to find myself in the midst of the bloodiest scenes of violence and of outrage, however earnestly I strove to gain that solitude and serenity which literature alone can offer."

They were camped in a cave by the side of a river, perhaps eight miles from the scene of Peter's rescue. Mr. Paddock was sitting sedately on a large boulder close to a fire which Donald Oge had lit. He had removed his oversized beaver hat which he now held primly upon his knees for all the world as if he were sitting in some Boston parlor and somewhat concerned about the impression he was making on his hosts.

"When I parted with you before the Battle of King's Mountain," he continued, "I suffered the most wretched depression of spirit, viewing my own timidity and contrasting it with your courage. Why, I asked myself, must I live out my life trembling in the face of violence? Was it not possible, I wondered, to screw up some courage in myself and risking all, perform some deed of valor which would atone for that unmanliness which has dogged me all my days?

"In my wanderings in the wilderness with my traveling university, I met several gentlemen interested in literature who, in private conversation, confessed that they themselves were quite as timid as I. They might read with every animation of spirit those magnificent accounts of the deeds of the heroes of old. But faced themselves with a demand for physical courage and prowess, they were utterly fearful. They also possessed a strong desire to perform some deed which might admit them to manhood and atone for their previous years.

"Quite without any organization at all, these gentlemen joined me—a band, sir, of men rendered desperate by their very lack of resolution. You see them about you now." He waved his hand around to indicate perhaps a dozen men, the greater number of them elderly and frail of physique. They bobbed their heads at Peter, acknowledging the introduction.

"We had arms but were afraid to show them," continued Mr. Paddock. "We hid them in my cart and the load being too much for Aesop, had to leave out some of my books, which were put in a safe place not far from Camden. The decision to do this caused me great pain," added Mr. Paddock, "and I might add that the pain was greatly aggravated by the thought that if it were found I was carrying firearms rather than books in my cart, I would certainly be hung and so would these other gentlemen who followed me.

"We had no plan at all except to keep in touch— though at a safe distance—with yourself and your raiders. We had a desire to perform some valiant deed, but when the opportunity for valor presented itself, we were not equal to the occasion. Thus, by common consent, we took no part in the battle of Cowpens, but rather lay shivering a mile and a half away across the river, our hands clapped to our ears to keep out the sound of the conflict.

"After the battle we thought we might assist the surgeon who had been left by General Morgan with the wounded and presented ourselves. It was then that I learned of your capture and we decided that here was the test and opportunity we required. We decided, in short, that we must rescue you."

The memory of this decision produced such an effect on Mr. Paddock that the perspiration broke out on his brow and he mopped his face vigorously with a large handkerchief which he produced from the pocket of his coat.

"Actually I decided that we ought to do this," he continued, "and to my horror the others agreed with me. I assure you that I immediately repented my rashness and begged them to consider whether we were not being foolhardy and running into a danger which we could readily avoid. They all agreed that this was the case and that we should not rescue you at all, since the thing might not be accomplished without more courage than we collectively possessed. But that night, when we retired, I could not sleep and neither could any of these gentlemen here. Our consciences troubled us deeply. We had, in fact, confirmed the judgment that we had already passed on ourselves—we had collectively acknowledged cowardice when given an opportunity to display a little courage. It was more than we could tolerate. We decided then, fearful though we were, that we must attempt your rescue."

"Before you go on," said Peter, "tell why it was that you decided to rescue me rather than some other prisoners."

"That is simply explained," said Mr. Paddock. "You are young, strong, vigorous and bold and a natural leader of men. We are the opposite—elderly, somewhat weak, lacking in resolution and timid. If men such as we could rescue one such as you to continue the glorious struggle for liberty, we would feel that we had justified our existence upon earth. There was, I confess, one more factor. You are the only partisan leader to our knowledge familiar with the works of Shakespeare. How could we let such a man be hung, diminishing in some degree the light of learning in this terrible wilderness? That I assure you was a factor in our decision." The others nodded their agreement.

"The decision made, we left Cowpens where we were able to secure horses from those which, after the battle, returned riderless to the scene of action, and followed after Cornwallis. They expected no enemy to the rear and so we had little difficulty in following. We encouraged each other by reciting the more vigorous parts of Henry V, particularly that glorious passage by the King before Harfleur.

"'Once more unto the breach, dear friends, once more . . .'"—"'Or pile the wall up with our English dead. . . .'" recited Peter.

"Precisely," said Mr. Paddock. "The rest is readily told. Tarleton, bringing up the rear, remained a little behind the main army to hang you. We tied Aesop to a tree, each took a musket and a knife and at the moment when you were about to receive your dismissal, fired upon the Redcoats and in the disorder that ensued, cut you down and brought you and your friend away."

It was Donald Oge who broke the silence that followed. "It was a brave deed and the work of gentlemen," he said. "It is a relief to me that I do not owe my life to some ploughman or merchant or servant but to men of books. I will shake your hand, sir, and thank you and you may say that you are the friend of Donald Oge Farqueson."

"You are yourself a man of letters?" asked Mr. Paddock while his hand was being vigorously pumped by Donald Oge.

"I am not," said Donald Oge. "I cannot write my own name but there is a chieftain's blood in my veins and I do not need to learn to lay the clerk."

"I will gladly teach you to write and to read as well," said Mr. Paddock.

"As to reading," said Donald Oge, "I prefer a story that is told to me. But I would like to know how to write my name. I would like to see what it looks like in letters. It is in my mind that it should look very handsome indeed."

"And so it would," said Mr. Paddock. "Very handsome indeed and especially if written in your own hand."

They ate a meal together and then came a discussion among Mr. Paddock's men about what should be done next. All were of the opinion that they had achieved what they aimed at and should return now to their homes. But Mr. Paddock wanted to go with Peter and Peter welcomed the offer.

"I can promise you no more courage," said Mr. Paddock, "for I believe I have used up every scrap I am entitled to for the rest of my life."

"I will not ask courage of you," said Peter. "Your counsel will be all that is required."

So it was agreed. The party split up and Peter, Donald Oge and Mr. Paddock set out to the north to meet Peter's men whom Donald Oge had left under McClintock's charge. Reunited they made a big circle to the north and east to pass Clinton and catch up as best they could with Morgan and Greene.

*19* ☆

King's Mountain had been fought in October of 1780 and Cowpens in January of 1781. In the days that followed General Greene won the race to the Dan River, saving his army for a further battle by getting over that huge and flooded stream into Virginia. There, rested and reinforced, he turned and gave battle to Cornwallis, at Guildford Courthouse.

Outnumbered, Greene lost the battle but as Nolli-chucky Jack said to Peter Treegate afterwards, "It was the best defeat we ever suffered, and the worst victory Cornwallis ever won. He cannot afford another one."

Peter was surprised at the remark. He and his Raiders, before the actual battle, had kept hitting at Cornwallis' army in lightening strikes and they had been in the forefront of the battle and knew that Greene's losses were heavy.

"Cornwallis' were heavier," said Nollichucky. "We can be reinforced. We had enlisted new men. But he cannot."

"And why not?" asked Peter.

"The only reinforcements he can get are from England or from Clinton in New York. Clinton will hardly dare send men to Cornwallis lest Washington attack New York. And to get more men from England will take several months. I think we are beginning to see the end of this affair."

Peter shook his head. "We have struck no blow hard enough to mortally hurt the British," he said.

"It is the little blows that count in the long run," said Nollichucky. "Added together they exhaust the Redcoats. Things will change and sooner than you think."

Peter did not believe him. He had been on active service in the field with his men for six months and was weary. He would have been glad of a rest—glad to get back to Salem and call on Peace of God Manly and his daughter Nancy. His thoughts turned more often to her lately. But he could not apply for leave since his own men had had none and there was no prospect of getting any for several months.

There was nothing to do but to hang on—to keep fighting and getting away and fighting again with no end in sight as far as he could see.

Far away to the north and east the big and enduring man who commanded the American army was feeling the weariness of the war also. Washington had been heartened by the news of King's Mountain and of Cowpens and disturbed by the report of Greene's defeat at Guildford Courthouse. He also awaited the one big blow, the one climatic battle which would secure victory in this war which had dragged on now for an impossible five years.

The problems were the same as they had been at the outset—an insufficient army insufficiently armed. He had hoped that all would change with the arrival of the French as allies. But the first French fleet sent had got itself hopelessly bottled up at Newport and could not gain the seas again. And a second French fleet, commanded by de Grasse, had sailed not for the American continent but to the West Indies, there to harass British shipping and British colonies. There was a vague promise that de Grasse would leave the West Indies in midsummer of the year 1781 and co-operate with Washington in an attack on New York. But there was nothing firm about this prospect and the French troops—excellent regiments—stationed round Newport could hardly be said to have fired a shot in anger in two years.

There was then a stalemate in New England and a stalemate in the southern colonies. The only field of action was in Virginia where the turncoat Arnold had been sent to the Chesapeake to ravage the countryside. Washington had countered the move by dispatching the young French nobleman, La Fayette, with a small force. There were signs that the British were building up their effort in the Chesapeake area though with what purpose Washington could not clearly see. Perhaps to link with Cornwallis for an attack through Virginia.

Washington sent Anthony Wayne with the Pennsylvania line to reinforce La Fayette. But he could spare few men. The big scene of action he was still convinced would be New York. He could not much reduce his army which was keeping watch on the city. And so spring became summer and the bright new leaves along the Hudson Valley took on a deeper green and became covered with dust. The days and weeks rolled by and the tall patient man waited for news from the French Admiral de Grasse, far away in the West Indies. On that news, it now seemed, all would depend.

Peace of God Manly sat in the tiny cabin of the Sloop of War *Defiance* writing a letter to his daughter, Nancy, in Salem. His ship, after making a cruise from Salem to the West Indies, had become attached to the huge French fleet under Admiral de Grasse, to be used both as a picket vessel and a messenger. On picket duty, it was Peace of God's task to patrol just over the horizon from the main body of the French, keeping an eye open for any strange sail and signaling immediately as one was sighted. As a messenger he was sent to one or other of the French West Indian Islands with instructions for the garrison there from the Admiral. But now the *Defiance* was at anchor with the rest of the French in the harbor of Martinique and Peace of God had time to write to his daughter.

His letter was a composite of news of the ship, instructions on the management of the small farm in Salem, and exhortations to his daughter to be at all times seemly in her behavior, remembering that the Lord was ever present, watching her actions and reading her innermost thoughts.

"I have much trouble with Master Gunner Simmons in these parts," wrote Peace of God forming each letter as carefully as a child at work in a copybook. "The devil's brew of rum is ever in his thoughts and it is only the great mercy of God, who loves all sinners, that he has not been struck down for his iniquities which ravish the body while destroying the mind. He hath a plentitude of boils about his arms and chest and face from rum drinking yet does his work manfully so that if he could be brought to the Lord, he would be like a Gideon in the army of the saved.

"There should be a run of mackerel toward the end of July. The best place to take them is between the rock known as the Barrel of Beef and the Nag's Head. There are three small casks of salt in the attic and these should be got ready to salt down the catch, and they may fetch four shillings the hundredweight in the Boston market. It is right to get a fair price but do not ask more than is just, for what the Lord sends freely from the depths of the ocean is not to be put to the use of avarice. Four shillings the hundredweight would be a seemly price but if four shillings and sixpence be offered, that may be taken. If five shillings is offered do not sell at so high a price, but at the lower figure for it is sinful to receive that much for salted mackerel at any time. Put aside one cask of them for thine own use during the winter when the fishing will likely be poor.

"The *Defiance* is now well trimmed, but fights her helm on the starboard tack when held close. She had three new ribs set to starboard and new planking where the worm had got in but it was not done right and hath somewhat spoiled her line along the sheer strakes. I have moved two of the eightpounders two feet aft for running. Before she put her head down too hard and now she does as well before the wind as any brig from Salem. The crew is well trained and serve handily except for swearing, but this, with God's help, I try to remedy with prayer meeting during the evening watch and the singing of hymns and psalms. I get along tolerable well with the French, though they be foreign and great wine drinkers. Yet they are but poor wretched sinners as I am myself and I have no right to make any judgement on them and ask God's pardon for so doing.

> Your loving father,
> Peace of God Manly."

When he had written this, Peace of God put down the quill pen and wiped off the end of his long nose on which a drop of perspiration had gathered. The cabin was unmercifully hot. Rain had fallen an hour before —the sudden thundering rain of the tropics. Now the sun was shining in full power and between the heat and humidity and the closeness of the air, his cabin was intolerable. He looked over the letter he had written, sanded it and then sealed it with a wafer which was soggy with moisture. It would have to be given to the censor on the Admiral's flagship before being dispatched by whatever ship of the fleet sailed for an American port.

As he left the cabin to go on deck, his first officer, Ephraim Coverly, who was from the town of Mystic, hailed him. "There's a signal flying from the Frenchy's foremast," he said.

Ephraim Coverly did not like the French, largely because they were French and not New Englanders. He was of the opinion that they were not seamen at all, and worked their ships like so many New Yorkers. He had a poor opinion of New Yorkers too, or indeed of anyone who did not come from Massachusetts.

"What signal?" asked Peace of God.

"Blue Peter, Yellow Jack and the other's just going up. . . . Letter A." said Ephraim. Through a telescope he was watching the signal flags being hoisted to the foretopmast yard of the Admiral's flagship.

"That means he wants us to send a boat," said Peace of God. Ephraim eyed him suspiciously. If Peace of God took over the watch, he Ephraim Coverly of Mystic would have to visit the Frenchy Admiral and he did not like the idea at all. Peace of God understood the look.

"Lower the whaler," he said. "I'll go over myself."

"Choice of cox'n, sir?" asked Ephraim.

Peace of God hesitated. Simmons was the best coxswain to handle the tiller. But if Simmons got alongside the Frenchman he would, though speaking not a word of French, manage in some magical way to coax someone to hand him a bottle of wine or rum through one of the gunports.

"I'll take her myself, Mr. Coverly," said Peace of God. The boat was lowered and, with Peace of God at the tiller, went smartly over to the huge 120-gun *Ville de Paris* which was the flagship of Admiral de Grasse.

The Admiral received Peace of God in his great cabin and alone. The cabin was so big that it seemed it could hold quite readily the little brig *Defiance* which Peace of God commanded. It was ornately decorated with the supporting posts carved with gilded cherubs peeping from behind carved, silvered roses. There was a large tapestry hung on one of the bulkheads depicting a scene from Greek mythology which Peace of God pronounced afterward to be "heathen, sinful and an offense to Christian men."

He forced himself to keep his eyes on de Grasse who was seated at a large carved desk of teakwood.

"Captain Manly reporting in answer to your signal, sir," he said.

De Grasse smiled—a pleasant friendly smile. He had heard of this sea captain from Salem whose fighting career had brought him fame in France and whose devotion to the saving of souls was the talk of the French fleet.

"Sit down, Captain Manly," he said in excellent English. "A glass of wine?"

"No thank'ee, sir," said Peace of God. And he added, "It is a device of Satan's." Whether de Grasse heard this or not, he chose to ignore it.

"How fast do you think you can fetch Boston, Captain Manly?" the Admiral asked.

"Twelve days armed," said Peace of God. "Ten days if I put my guns ashore—God sending a fair wind, which would be likely at this time of the year, though it would be presumptuous to rely upon it and sinful too."

"If you put your guns ashore, will you need to shift your ballast?" asked the Admiral.

"I will, sir," said Peace of God. "I'll need to move a ton from amidships to the butt of the foremast or she will drag her stern deep in the water. Half a day would do it. Half a day to get the guns ashore and half a day to move ballast."

De Grasse nodded, took a sheet of paper and handed it to Peace of God. "These are your orders to leave for Boston on a special mission," he said. "They are in French but that is what they say. You will make for Boston, Philadelphia or New London, or any port on the American coast at which you can dock, and then proceed to the Commander-in-Chief of the Continental Forces with a special message from me. What is essential is that you deliver the message and with the greatest possible speed."

Peace of God nodded. He was beginning to think the Frenchman sensible in that he had picked the *Defiance* to carry the message for she could outsail any vessel in the fleet, including the smaller French frigates at the Admiral's disposal. And it was right to put his guns ashore for he could not afford to engage in any action with an enemy vessel if he had an important message to deliver.

"You'll have the message written out, sir?" he asked.

For answer de Grasse took a sheet of paper and stamped it in the middle with a huge stamp on the desk before him. He signed his name through the stamp mark and gave the paper to Peace of God who examined it puzzled.

"This is the message, sir?" he asked.

"No," said de Grasse. "That is merely the guarantee of its veracity. The message you will deliver verbally to no one but General Washington. And you will deliver it to him when he is alone as I am now." Peace of God nodded, and waited.

"The message is that I will leave here in two weeks and my destination will be Chesapeake Bay. He may expect me in a month at the latest. You are not to write this message down nor repeat it to anyone but General Washington. When you have repeated it to him, you will forget about it entirely. May I put complete reliance on you in this regard?"

"You may, sir," said Peace of God soberly.

"Good," said de Grasse. "On the safe delivery of this message and on its being kept absolutely secret may well depend the whole future of your country's struggle for freedom. You may sail when you are ready. And good luck."

They shook hands and Peace of God returned to the *Defiance*. He ordered her warped alongside the dock and there to the disgust of Simmons, her guns were off-loaded and her ballast redistributed so as to trim the ship properly. Peace of God rowed twice around her himself, inspecting her waterline when this was done, to see that she lay well in the water.

This work went on through the remainder of the day and well into the morning of the following day. Then about eleven o'clock, all being ready, the *Defiance* hoisted her topsails and hauled her yards around for a long run with the trade wind for the American colonies. As she cleared the headland a single farewell shot boomed out from the huge *Ville de Paris* and then the little brig was lost in the blue tropical haze.

## 20

It was August now—the August of 1781—a terrible hot
New England August when not a leaf stirred and the
very sky seemed to have weight and to press down upon
the earth and the people below. The Hudson seemed a
river of molten metal flowing between glowering banks.
There was a shimmer of heat upon everything. It rose
from the tents around Washington's headquarters—
tents which were insufferable in the daytime and hardly
habitable at night. It rose from the roof of the big ugly
mansion where the Commander-in-Chief lived and it
quivered off the overlush grasslands and woods around.

A multitude of summer flies bedeviled the soldiers,
buzzed against the tent walls, against window panes
and hung in clouds over the horses whose tails were

busy swishing them away from dawn to dusk. When dark came the flies went to be replaced by clouds of mosquitoes. Everyone was made fretful by the flies, the mosquitoes and the unending heat, but most of all by the sense of waiting.

The men did not really know what they were waiting for. They had earlier in the summer been reinforced by the French from Newport and presumed that they would attack New York lower down the river. But nothing happened. They just waited in the heat by the river that seemed full of molten metal—waited for some decisive order that would come—but no one knew when.

Only one man knew what the waiting was about and he was a man long endured to patience. George Washington was waiting for news from de Grasse. July had gone and de Grasse had not appeared off the American coast and was still presumably in the West Indies. De Grasse must send news some time, saying he was either staying in the West Indies or was coming to New York so that the great attack upon New York City could be undertaken.

And yet de Grasse was silent and the only news was that the British concentrations on the Chesapeake were being strengthened. Cornwallis had withdrawn to Wilmington in North Carolina after the battle of Guildford Courthouse. There he had been reinforced and had struck north into Virginia, crossing the Dan unopposed. He was linking up with the forces under Arnold.

What was this? A bluff—or a real attack into the northern area from the south? Was it a strategy to draw Washington and his army away from New York? Or was it a serious threat to the middle colonies.

Washington had sent La Fayette instructions to try to contain the British around the Chesapeake. Wayne would join La Fayette soon. Together their joint forces would be inferior to those of the British, but this was the best that could be done until Washington received news from de Grasse.

So he waited for news through the heat of July and through the first two weeks of August. And then on the fourteenth of August news came.

On that day Peace of God Manly arrived at Washington's headquarters on a horse white with sweat and demanded to see the Commander-in-Chief personally. An attempt was made to divert him to General Edward Hand, Washington's aide de camp. But Peace of God was insistent that his news was urgent and could be delivered to the Commander-in-Chief only. He would say in extension merely that he came from the West Indies, and when General Hand heard this, he took Peace of God to the General's office and brought him in.

"A courier, sir," he said, "from the West Indies."

Washington was writing at a table and when he heard the words "West Indies" he flung down his pen and came quickly from behind the desk. "What is it?" he asked in such excitement that he did not bother to inquire the name of the messenger nor his rank, nor question his credentials.

"I can only speak to you alone, sir," said Peace of God.

"What are your credentials?" asked General Hand suspiciously, for there had been many attempts by assassins to gain a few moments alone with the Commander-in-Chief.

"Those I can show to you," said Peace of God and reaching into the pocket in the tail of his sea coat drew out a crumpled piece of paper much dampened by perspiration and perhaps ocean water. There had been a seal on the paper but this was now broken. Hand noted the broken seal with suspicion, opened the piece of paper and handed it without a word to Washington.

"De Grasse?" cried Washington. "De Grasse? You come from him?"

"I do," said the other. "My name being Peace of God Manly. One of Wesley's flock of poor sinners."

This astonishing introduction was lost on General Washington for the moment. He gestured to Hand to leave and as soon as the door had shut behind him said, "Your news! Your news! What message had de Grasse for me?"

"He will be off the Chesapeake in two weeks' time with twenty-four ships of the line," said Peace of God.

"The Chesapeake?" cried Washington. "Are you sure the Chesapeake? Not the Hudson?"

"The Chesapeake," repeated Peace of God. Then he added, "Begging your pardon, sir, not even a Frenchman would be foolish enough to take a war fleet into the narrow waters of the Hudson where it could be bottled up by four frigates."

But Washington was not listening. He went hurriedly to his desk, pulled out several maps from a drawer and after hastily examining them, threw three on the floor while he concentrated on a fourth which he unrolled on his desk. It was a map of area around Chesapeake Bay.

His whole strategy for the conduct of the war had to be changed but he had been presented with a glorious chance to achieve victory. Here was Cornwallis and the men whom Arnold had commanded, though Arnold had now been withdrawn from the scene. Before him was the thin little army of La Fayette and at his back was the sea. Undoubtedly Cornwallis believed that he could, if need be, evacuate his army by sea. But if de Grasse sailed into Chesapeake Bay, Cornwallis would be cut off. And de Grasse had sent a message that he would be arriving in the Chesapeake in a fortnight. Nothing could be more fortuitous. If La Fayette could hold Cornwallis until Washington could march to reinforce him, the British commander was doomed. He would be beseiged by land and by sea and must surrender. It was as if de Grasse had foreseen the whole situation and even planned it.

Where would Cornwallis be likely to make his stand? Washington scanned the map carefully and came on the name of a little village, so small that it was written only in the tiniest type. The name was Yorktown—a pleasant English sounding name that Cornwallis himself had noted some months before when in the wilderness of the Carolinas.

Yorktown. That was the likeliest place. And now Washington had to rush his army down to reinforce La Fayette, take command himself, and hope for a victory.

Washington raised his big face, red with excitement, from the map he had been studying. His breath was coming sharply, such was the extent of his emotion.

"This is the greatest stroke of fortune to come our way since the start of the war," he said.

"For which thanks be to God without Whom all is to no purpose," said Peace of God. Washington stared at him for a moment and then said soberly, "That is true. For which thanks be to God." He rang the bell on his desk sharply and when General Hand appeared started to give him his orders. He gave them crisply and without hesitation and what they amounted to was the concentration of all American and French forces around the village of Yorktown, Virginia, on the south shore of Chesapeake Bay.

The Franco-American army that now plunged southward, raising a pall of dust over its route through New Jersey and Pennsylvania made a column two miles long. Brigadier General Henry Knox, who had sold books in Boston before the war, led three regiments of artillery which he had trained himself, largely out of his reading. There were foot regiments from Massachusetts and Connecticut and New Jersey and Rhode Island. There was the famous Delaware Regiment which had seen action on every major field during the war, and more of the Pennsylvanians going to join Mad Anthony Wayne, their commander who was already with La Fayette. And following these came the famous regiments of France, that of Bourbonnois and of Soissonois and Saintoge, Agenois, Gatenois and Touraine with the cavalry of the Duke de Lauzun and the Artillery of d'Aboville.

The ground shook under the wheels of the cannon and the tramping of feet. The French looked gay in their blue coats and white stockings and breeches. The Americans were more drab, for though each regiment of the Continental Line technically had its own uniform, few had ever been issued to the men. The Delawares managed to sport a few green hunting shirts and the Pennsylvanians a few of the official black. But for the most part the Americans were clad in whatever clothing they could find—some in deerskins and some in worsted. Yet they had about them the look of veterans and the French found cause to admire the tirelessness of their marching and the manner in which they could, in a few minutes, get a meal for themselves out of the most meager supplies. They were veterans indeed, these Americans, and many a professional French officer remarked that they were probably some of the best troops to be found anywhere in the world.

This march, the greatest mass movement of troops in the whole of the Revolutionary War, commenced on the 19th of August and the combined American and French Armies were at Williamsburg ready for the assault on Cornwallis at Yorktown by the 27th of September. The distance covered was over four hundred miles and the Hudson and Delaware Rivers had to be crossed, accounting for much of the delay. Other troops moved up from the south, sent by General Greene who remained to watch the British garrisons left in the Carolinas by Cornwallis. Peter Treegate, now promoted from Captain to Major for his part in the critical battles of King's Mountain and Cowpens, marched north with the former force. Treegate's men reached La Fayette before the main army from the north and helped contain Cornwallis until Washington arrived. And then Treegate sought out Wayne with a special request.

"We have an old grudge against Tarleton," he said. "We would think it a favor if we could be put in that part of the line opposite Tarleton and his legion."

"If there is a man in the South who has not got a grudge against Tarleton, I have yet to hear of him," said Wayne.

"Tarleton had the impertinence to attempt to hang me," said Donald Oge. "As a gentleman you will see that it is necessary to wipe out that insult."

Wayne laughed. "So be it," he said. "When we find out the disposition of the enemy, you may take your place in the line opposite Tarleton's Legion."

The attack, or rather the seige of Yorktown started on the next day. The Franco-American Army marched eleven miles from Williamsburg to place themselves before Yorktown and found that Cornwallis had thrown up works outside the village from which to conduct his defense. But two days later came a surprise. Donald Oge went forward with a little patrol before dawn to reconnoiter the enemy's trenches and returned in a state of excitement.

"They're empty!" he said. "There's not a man in them! The Redcoats have run to the inner defenses and left their trenches to us."

This proved to be the case. A few patrols were sent over to see if all the British trenches had been evacuated and then the beseiging army moved forward and occupied them. The ring around Yorktown was tightened and it would be tightened more and more in the days that followed.

To Donald Oge's disgust there was however no assault on the British lines. He had hoped for a pitched battle fought to a bloody conclusion. He found that instead the engineers busied themselves constructing a further line of trenches, closer to the British and learned from Peter that when these were complete they would be occupied.

"And what then?" demanded Donald Oge.

"Then another line will be built even closer," replied Peter.

"But this isn't fighting at all," stormed Donald Oge. "It is burrowing like moles. I would be ashamed to go back to my father and tell him that we had beaten the Sassenachs by digging in the ground."

"When the last line has been built," said Peter, "the big siege guns will be mounted in them in batteries and will batter down the British defenses. And then we will go forward to attack."

Donald Oge was immediately interested, for he was always excited by cannon. He still had with him the small "grasshopper" field piece captured at Cowpens. He went now to inspect the big field pieces in the artillery train of Knox and of the French, which were being landed from barges on the river, and was enormously impressed by the size of them. He was impatient to see them fired and begged the artillery officers to discharge one for him. But he was told that they would not be put into action until in position, in the batteries under construction.

Up to this point he had been contemptuous of the seige lines. Now his attitude changed and he was impatient to have them finished, even volunteering to help dig them and put in place the sand bags and "fascines" of wickerwork with which they were protected.

"It will be the wonder of the world when those cannon are fired," he said to Peter. "The noise of them alone would knock down a house. There is one that is so big that a boy could slip down the barrel and it will throw shot weighing a hundred pounds."

The first parallel of seige lines was finished by the second week in October. The work was done under a consistent British bombardment and Peter and his men were given the job of protecting the engineers, picking off any of the enemy who exposed themselves. Then the big mortars and cannon were hauled into their places and Washington himself fired the first shot which opened the bombardment of Yorktown. Immediately the air was rent with explosions as guns from one end to the other of the Franco-American lines hurled their shot and shells at the British lines. The cannonade continued all day and all night to the joy of Donald Oge who begged Peter to allow him to serve with the gunners. Since there was little other work to do, Peter gave permission.

Meanwhile a second trench was started, even nearer to the British position and this was completely under cover of the artillery in a few days. Again the guns were moved forward, and though the British tried two sorties to spike them, the emplacements were maintained.

On the morning of October 17th with the American cannonade still continuing, a lone drummer climbed to the top of the British works and started to beat a parley on his drum. Peter saw him—a little figure in red, standing firmly at attention, beating away vigorously—and marveled that he was not killed. Gradually, without anyone saying a word, the cannonade died down. In the appalling silence that followed all that could be heard was the beating of the drum by the lone drummer scarcely four hundred yards away. An officer waving a white handkerchief in his hand mounted behind the drummer boy. Wayne was standing beside Peter and said to him, "Go forward and bring that officer over here. But blindfold him first."

Peter felt his heart pounding heavily as he sprinted over to the British officer. Surely, he thought, this cannot be the end? It cannot finish like this—one lone drummer boy beating his drum and one lone British officer standing beside him with a white handkerchief in his hand.

What was it Nollichucky Jack had said to him—years ago it seemed? "One day we will have the right number of men in the right place at the right time and then it will be all over." Something like that. And now it had come to pass though it seemed a dream.

He was soon beside the British officer but looked first at the drummer boy because he was so small and so soldierly. He was fair-haired and had not even a trace of down on his face. He stood perfectly "at ease" as if on parade. He could not have been more than twelve years of age, and was very thin.

"My son," said the officer, seeing Peter so interested in the boy. "His first engagement and I regret that we have lost." There was a glint of tears in the boy's eyes but no other expression.

"Your name and rank?" asked Peter.

"Major John Pettifield, 18th Lincolnshire Regiment of Foot. And yours?"

"Major Peter Treegate of the Pennsylvania Line."

"Treegate of Treegate's Raiders?" asked Major Pettifield.

Peter nodded. The other held out his hand. "You are a man of some valor and reputation, sir," he said.

"What is the purpose of the parley?" asked Peter.

"The appointment of commissioners to discuss terms of surrender," said Major Pettifield.

Peter produced a scarf. "I must blindfold you to take you through our works," he said. The other nodded and submitted while the scarf was tied over his eyes.

Then Peter led him by the hand toward the American lines. The drummer boy remained standing on the parapet, his drum silent. The tears now showed plainly on his face.

Thinking about it later, Peter Treegate was always struck that the war which had dragged on so long and seemed so many times completely hopeless should have ended with such a small and intimate incident. He had somehow come to believe that there would be a massive engagement of armies on some field and that a great battle would be won or lost and this would be the finish. But it ended instead in silence when the drummer boy, having beaten his request for a parley, thrust his drumsticks into the front of his red tunic and all noise drained away from Yorktown and its environs.

What followed afterward seemed to Peter a complete anticlimax. On the 19th of October, 1781, in the early afternoon, the British filed out of Yorktown. The French stood on one side of the road, the Americans on the other. The local people from the surrounding countryside were not allowed to watch, and there was a respectful silence among the ranks at this spectacle of the surrender of the King's proud army. The French were turned out with new black elastic garters to wrap around their white gaiters to present as smart an appearance as possible. But there was no new gear for the men of the Continental Army. They did not even bother to dress ranks properly, but lined up regiment by regiment in a loose manner for they had never had any love of drill for the sake of drill, and even the presence of General Washington would not persuade them to put on a smarter show.

Washington inspected the lines of troops before the British marched out and looking at the smartly dressed and drilled French on one side and the ragged Continentals on the other he smiled. The men saw him smile and cheered, so that he blushed. Then he pushed his horse into a canter to take up his position for the surrender.

Peter's men had been assigned a position at the end of the American column—that is at the end nearest to the British lines and they watched as the British and

Hessian officers came out first, led by General O'Hara, aide to Cornwallis, who stated that Cornwallis himself was too ill to surrender in person. O'Hara first tried to offer his sword to Rochambeau, the French commander, but was signaled to give it to General Washington as Commander-in-Chief. O'Hara then offered his sword to Washington who said with great sincerity, "Never from so good a hand," and refused to take the sword from him. It was finally surrendered to Washington's aide, General Lincoln.

But Peter's men were waiting for one particular officer—Banastre Tarleton. He came in the main group immediately behind O'Hara and Donald Oge, seeing him, shouted "Tarleton! Tarleton! Over here! We have your own quarter for you."

Tarleton turned, saw Donald and Peter and the grim men around them. Donald Oge was holding a rope with a hangman's noose at one end. Tarleton's face went white and he moved his horse away and conferred quickly with another officer. Then he cantered down the line and surrendered to a French officer under whose protection, Peter learned later, he placed himself, saying that he was afraid if he fell into the hands of the Americans, he would be hung for his misdeeds.

Then came the British regiments, scowling and marching poorly, their band playing deliberately out of tune. The Germans marched better bringing up the rear. They went to a big field where they laid down their arms. Then the dust settled on the quiet road leading to Yorktown and all was over.

## 21

The run of mackerel off the New England coast, which had started early in August, had continued until late in September so that Nancy Manly had taken, with the help of neighbors, enough to fill ten casks when salted. Four of these had been sent on a cart to the market in Boston with instructions to the carter that they were to be sold at no greater price than four and sixpence the hundredweight. The rest had been kept back, one to be used during the winter and the others to be sold at a later date when the glut was over. After the mackerel there had been a dearth of fish and Nancy was engaged in preparing handlines for the cod season during the winter when her father came back from the war.

He wrote no letter in advance and, deeming it sinful to hire a horse or buy a seat even on the outside of a coach, he walked from Boston to Salem, occasionally stopping in a village to gather a few people together and "humbly comfort them in their toils with a few words from Holy Writ." So he was two weeks on the road from Boston to Salem and when he walked through the door of his cottage, found his daughter knotting cod hooks onto the heavy lines that would be used in the coming fishing.

"Four feet apart is best for early cod," he said as he came through the door and saw her at the work. "Late cod will shoal. . . ." Whatever else he was going to say went unspoken for his daughter gave a little cry and rushed to embrace him and then, to his surprise, started weeping.

"What's fretting thee?" said Peace of God. "Is aught wrong?"

"You're back and safe," she said and could only repeat this over and over through her tears.

"So God willed it," said Peace of God. "And had He willed otherwise it would have been only His great mercy toward us, though hard for us in our foolishness to understand."

She made him sit down, hushed his further sermonizing and, a kettle being on the hob, made a dish of tea from a little she had saved against this very day, screwed up in a piece of brown paper and put upon the mantlepiece. Her father, she knew, denied himself every kind of luxury. But he had a weakness for a big strong dish of tea and she made him take it though he said that it was more than he deserved and he would repent such waste later.

Then she got control of herself and sat in the chair opposite him and tried to go on with the business of tying hooks on the line. But she could not concentrate on it and put aside the work and sat on the floor beside him, her head in his lap.

"Why," said Peace of God. "You are a grown woman and yet you are like a little child and in need of comfort every minute. It is a mystery to me, though I remember your mother was much the same way, particularly in a northeast gale."

"Father," said Nancy, "there are no grown women nor grown men, but only children who have to look after each other."

To this Peace of God said nothing for the thought had never occurred to him before and so he had nothing to say to it.

After a little while Nancy asked, "How is Master Gunner Simmons?" Her father did not reply immediately, but heaved a great sigh eloquent of a heavy sorrow.

"He is lost," he said at length. "I have done all I may for him and spent hours praying for him and pleading with him to save his soul. But he could not resist the snares of Satan and he is lost."

"He's dead?" asked Nancy.

Peace of God shook his head. "Not dead," he said. "Worse. Married. Married to a certain Mistress Bridges of Boston who keeps a tavern called 'The Gunner's Rest.' There was nought I could do to prevent it. So Satan has entrapped him at last, and in his guile used the sacrament of marriage to supply Master Simmons with those liquors which will prove his ruination and send his soul into the pit of hell."

"I am not so sure that will be the case," said Nancy thoughtfully. "What kind of a woman is this Mistress Bridges?"

"A formidable woman, though it is wrong of me to say so. She has a voice like a brass cannon and I saw her myself throw out of her tavern two sailors who ordered a dram of rum apiece and having drunk it refused to pay."

"Then it may be that Master Gunner Simmons has found his salvation rather than his ruin in her," said Nancy. "For what you were unable to achieve by prayer, she may be able to achieve with discipline. I think the Master Gunner will be hard put to overindulge with Mistress Bridges around."

"That man could get rum or spirits of some sort from under the nose of an admiral and a guard of marines," said Peace of God firmly.

"But not from under the nose of Mistress Bridges, unless I am very much mistaken in her," said Nancy firmly. "And now tell me, have you any news of Captain Treegate." She tried to make the question sound idle but even her father was not deceived.

"None," he said. "None since he left here. He has not written you while I was at sea?"

"No."

"Then it may be that he has forgotten about us. It would not be just to blame him, for he was brought up wildly on the frontier among the Scots. If he is not dead, I think he will have gone back to the mountain valleys where he spent his boyhood."

"Perhaps he will still come," said Nancy though in a small voice. "He stood very tall and was hard and fierce and yet there was a gentleness in him too."

"Do not set your heart on his return, daughter," said Peace of God gently. "Do not set your heart on it." Then desperately searching for some way to change the subject he said, "I must look at the boat. I have been thinking about it and the knee below the forward thwart needs replacing before the winter sets in."

He got up and Nancy rose with him. "I will go with you," she said. "I have been here alone for a long time."

They went through the door together and round the corner of the cottage. The wind smote them briskly—an evening wind coming in fresh off the ocean. Nancy bent her head anticipating the blast and because of this she did not see the man who came running across the field towards them. He cleared a stone wall as readily as an antelope and shouted something but the words were snatched away in the wind. Then he was before her and picked her up, raising her above his head.

She looked down in fright and then said, "Peter . . . Peter. . . ." and it seemed that the whole world was made anew for her in that moment.

A month later Donald Oge led his men back into the valley of the Carolina mountains. They had taken six weeks in the journey from Yorktown for they were pulling with them, behind four draught horses, a seige mortar that fired a ten-inch shell. The mortar was put before the house of Donald Oge's father and it was fired once a year on the Fourth of July.

Some said this was to celebrate Independence Day but others argued that it was to symbolize the end of the feuds between the Farquesons and the Frasers and the Robertsons and the other clans around.

Only Donald Oge and McClintock knew that it celebrated both, for the one was part of the other and a new nation had been born out of diverse stocks and conditions of men. The men of the valleys who had been called Treegate's Raiders were part of a new nation now and would always be. The nation was called the United States of America and there were stars in its flag.

"That is a good augury," said Mr. Paddock, who had gone back with Donald Oge to teach him and others in the valley to read and write. "We aim at the stars, my friend. Some day we will achieve them. Meanwhile you should learn to write your name."

END OF THE FOURTH BOOK